Down to Earth

Andrew Crowther

Stairwell Books //

Published by Stairwell Books
161 Lowther Street
York, YO31 7LZ

www.stairwellbooks.co.uk
@stairwellbooks

Layout Alan Gillott
Cover design Alan Gillott
Cover Image from an image by Anton Gvozdikov

ISBN: 978-1-913432-59-1

p3

For Suzanne

Everything in this book is wrong.

CHAPTER ONE: Forever England

THAT NIGHT, JENNY STRAPPED HERSELF into her bed as usual and tried to sleep.

She wasn't a worrier, as a rule. She was happy to take life as it came, and life came to her happily. Still, that Sunday night, she lay awake with thoughts that would not stop. The new job loomed in her mind. Would she cope? Would she fit in? Would the children like her? Something lurched inside, and for a moment she felt, inexplicably, as if she were far from home, looking down on things from a strange high place like a tower. The feeling passed, and she was herself again. There in her room, she stared up through the cube of darkness and listened to the air beyond. She imagined she heard the faint faraway clack of the great slats. The curfew wagon rumbled down Empire Road and away into the distance. She smiled to herself. Yes, all was well. And, slowly, her mind emptied; her breathing softened; she slept.

In the morning, everything was, as it always is, altered. What had seemed terrifying at one o'clock was now almost welcoming. She woke in good humour, looking forward to the promise of the day. She unstrapped herself and floated out of bed, and even managed, for once, to get to the warm water before Mr Thark on the top floor. Scrubbed and pink, she chose the yellow spotted dress, with the daringly light shoes. It was a risk, but on a day like this, she wanted to tread lightly. She tripped down the street and arrived early, almost the first teacher through the gates.

The headmaster was Mr Jorrocks, large and red with a sweaty pate. He showed her round and introduced her to the teachers. "You will be shadowing Miss Jones for a few days, 'til you find your feet," he wheezed. "I'm sure you will take to it in no time. Like a fish," he added felicitously, "to water."

"How do you do," said Miss Jones. She was pale, tall, probably in her mid-fifties. At first sight she seemed most formidable, but when she looked frankly into Jenny's eyes and smiled, Jenny knew they would get on. "We have 2B at half past nine. They're a decent crowd, you'll like them."

Later, as she and Miss Jones walked down the empty corridor towards their class, she heard high voices in a far room chanting their lesson. "Amo, amas, amat. Amamus, amatis, amant." And all at once, Jenny was plunged back, small and innocent, into this same corridor as it had been, all those years ago.

"Sorry?" she said, recalled to the present.

"The class is down here."

"Oh, yes, I know the way. I was taught here."

Miss Jones smiled. "Oh dear, I hope it doesn't bring back bad memories."

"Indeed no, I enjoyed it."

They came to a room. Miss Jones said: "Here we are. We're doing the war poets today. One of my favourites."

"Oh, how lovely."

"Come on, let's set up."

The wooden desks were set in regimental rows. A long blackboard loomed behind the teacher's desk which was itself minutely elevated on a wooden dais. The King's portrait, solemn and froglike, hung next to the blackboard. All was as Jenny remembered; nothing, not one splinter on one desk, had changed.

Then, later:

"Good morning, class," said Miss Jones.

Twenty pink children responded in a solemn chorus: "Good morning, Miss Jones."

They sat in neat rows at their little desks, their uniforms crisp and clean (shorts for the boys, knee-length skirts for the girls), their white shins dangling, heartbreakingly young and vulnerable.

Miss Jones introduced Jenny: "This is Miss Threadneedle, and she will be your new teacher. I know you will make her very welcome. What do you say?"

"Good morning, Miss Fregneegle!"

"Good. Now class, turn to your books. Page 214."

The lesson proceeded. The emphasis was on Kipling, but towards the end Miss Jones turned to a more individual choice.

Without preamble, she opened the page and slowly read in her rich, precise voice:

> If I should die, think only this of me:
> That there's some corner of a foreign field
> That is for ever England.

She stopped, her eyes dim and remote. The pause lengthened, until Jenny was sure the children would grow restless. But they merely stared, devouring Miss Jones like maggots; and she proceeded. By the end, the class was in tears; Jenny too. She almost applauded.

"That poem. Does it have a special meaning for you?" Jenny asked afterwards.

"Yes," said Miss Jones, putting the books away. "Yes."

Jenny contributed more to the later lessons; in the afternoon, she taught 5C *Pride and Prejudice*, her favourite book. It all worked like a dream, and Jenny was walking on air until Miss Jones brought her down to earth with a bump. "I'm sorry," said Jenny. "I should have worn heavier shoes."

Afterwards, when the last bell had sounded and the last child had run home, Miss Jones looked at her and said, "You'll do fine."

As they tidied the classroom before departing, Jenny fell into a thoughtful silence. She glanced at Miss Jones.

3

"I hope you don't mind my asking..." she began.

"Of course not."

"Why are you leaving?"

Miss Jones continued with her work of straightening the desks.

"I'm fifty-four," she said at last.

"That's not old."

Miss Jones smiled at her. "Oh, bless you. Let's have a spot of tea somewhere. Then we can talk properly. There's a Lyons down the road."

At the Lyons Tea Shop, there was, inevitably, the gossiping pair seated by the window, the mournful young slip at the worst table munching her dry toast, the discreet man in the corner reading his paper. Jenny and Miss Jones were served with two lukewarm cups of brown water and, after some debate ("I can go as high as a shilling," Miss Jones said) two stale slices of Bakewell tart.

"Well?" challenged Jenny. "Why are you leaving really?"

Miss Jones considered. "People change. I've changed. I need to move on." She sipped her tea and pulled a face.

"Changed?" Jenny asked. "How?"

Miss Jones was evasive. "Oh, you know."

"I *don't* know. You're a good teacher. You make poetry live. Why aren't you staying?"

Jenny watched as Miss Jones came to a decision. Her light manner dropped from her and she looked at Jenny seriously and frankly. "Look here," she said. "Don't you ever feel you want to, to escape this whole charade?"

"What do you mean?"

Miss Jones saw her expression of honest surprise, and resumed the mask. "It doesn't matter."

"Yes, it does."

And now it was as if Miss Jones were drifting inside herself; and the steamy, grubby café dissolved into nothing. "We, I mean people... *homo sapiens,* for want of a better term... we're not one thing, ever. Each of us contains a multitude. You know Walt Whitman? No, of course you

4

don't. Well, every day we contradict what we think we know of ourselves. For years I thought all I wanted was security, safety, sameness. But now, quite at once, these questions come to me."

"Questions?"

"Like... what is all this *for*? Do I really want to die, here, in this most foreign field? And I find I am choking. Choking! *I have to get out*," she burst out with a sudden, frightening intensity.

"Out? Where to?"

"You don't understand a word I'm saying, do you?"

"I understand the words."

"But not the sentences? Well. You're much too young to... I suppose you've always lived here?"

"We came when I was almost three." Jenny had a flash of memory: the crowded chamber, the feeling of being crushed by the air itself, the noise that was almost physical.

"You don't remember much, then? Of before?"

Jenny considered. "Green. Rain. Birds."

"Yes. Not much, but perhaps enough. Well, I was thirty-three when I came here. So I remember."

"What do you remember?"

Miss Jones considered. "Variety," she said. "A universe of jumble. Shapes, sizes, accents, colours, all different. Black, brown, yellow, olive. As for the opinions... some of the opinions would make your hair curl!"

Jenny stirred in her seat, glancing around. "We shouldn't be talking of this..."

"No?... Oh, I knew perfectly well what it would be like here, even before I came. Stable. Unchanging. For ever and ever, amen. After all, it's what they planned. And it must have been what I wanted, once. But as it turns out... There are times when I look at the King's portrait, and I want to, to *spit* in his face. And right now, I would like more than anything to smash this stupid teacup... to run amok, and shatter for one moment this serene illusion, yes, and shout the most obscene things!... *Fuck the King! Bugger him to hell and back!*"

5

She had thrown the cup to the floor, where it bounced, and now she was on her feet, yelling madly, and with terrified eyes. The café was silent with embarrassment. No one was looking at them, deliberately, so that afterwards no one would say they had seen a thing. Only two people saw her, and one of them was Jenny, too shocked to look away.

As Jenny stared, Miss Jones broke off, leant towards her and whispered urgently: "Call the Police. Now!"

For a moment everything was a tangle in Jenny's head and she could do nothing. Then, as Miss Jones flashed a complicit smile and resumed her shouting, Jenny reached a decision and cried out: "Police!"

The man in the corner stood up, suddenly bigger and leaner than he had seemed, and strode over, the handcuffs glinting in his grasp.

CHAPTER TWO: Saturday Treats

ON WEEKDAYS, BREAKFAST AT MRS Cardigan's boarding house consisted of branny porridge and lucky to have it. However, come Saturday, and to mark the weekend, she would always try to provide something a little special. This week, it was corned meat fritters with beans.

Jenny was later than usual down to the breakfast table; so late, in fact, that she was only just ahead of Mr Thark.

"Ah, good morning, Miss Threadneedle," he said as he descended the last few steps. His smile was a crooked line in his sallow, baggy face. "I hope you're well? I haven't seen you for days."

"Yes, you won't have seen me at breakfast. I have to be at school by eight o'clock."

"How barbaric."

They took their seats at the table, the King looking down at them from his frame on the wall, and Mrs Cardigan doled out their portions. Jenny got extra beans.

For a time, the only sound was that of eating.

Mr Thark finished first, laying his knife and fork on the plate at the approved angle and leaning back with a replete sigh.

"And now," he said, once Jenny had also finished, "you must tell me all about your new job."

"What is there to say?" said Jenny.

"Well, what about the children? I am sure they are something appalling."

"Oh, no, they're sweet. You would love them, Mr Thark."

Mr Thark shuddered. "I know you're only teasing, but please don't. Grubby, mucus-filled homunculi. I shouldn't have brought the subject up. Tell me about the teachers. That should be more bearable. At least they have the virtue of adulthood."

"I like Mr Jorrocks the headmaster. They've all been very welcoming. Yes. Oh, but I must tell you about Miss Jones, that was very odd."

"Odd?" said Mr Thark, brightening up. "Yes, you must certainly tell me about the odd Miss Jones."

"I don't mean Miss Jones herself was odd... well, perhaps I do. It's just that I can't quite fathom the whole thing. I was with her all through my first day, and she was so clever and capable, and we seemed to be getting on so very well. And then, quite without warning... we were in the Lyons Tea Shop after school, and all at once she started shouting out the most awful things."

"Awful things? What kind of awful things?"

"I couldn't possibly repeat them, you mustn't ask me. They were just things about, you know, the King. Then the man in the corner came over and took her away."

"Yes," said Mr Thark, sipping his tea. "That certainly seems very odd. And yet, hasn't this kind of thing been happening quite a lot lately?"

"I wouldn't know about that, Mr Thark."

"No, perhaps not." Mr Thark wrote the "Tom Tattle" column in the *High Hants Gazette*, was in with the journalistic crowd, and often heard about events that the outside world never got to know of. "So she left you in the lurch on the first day?"

"I suppose you could say that, though she didn't mean to. What will they do to her?"

"Oh, kill her, I expect."

"Mr Thark!"

"Well, what else? But don't let's talk of her. How has your week been otherwise?"

"Everyone has been very helpful. I feel as if I've been at the school for positively years."

"Yes, school had that effect on me, too."

There was an awkward silence for a space, in the course of which Jenny hastened to finish her tea.

She hesitated a moment, then said:

"I'm popping over to see father this morning."

"Indeed? Well, give him my love."

"Oh, thank you, I will."

Mr Thark assumed she was about to leave, but to his surprise she remained seated, somehow giving the impression of staring at him while refusing to do so.

"Don't you," Mr Thark ventured, "usually go and see him on a Friday evening?"

"Yes. But what with being so busy all this week, I didn't have the time last night before curfew. So it will have to be today instead."

"I see."

Another pause.

"Mr Thark?"

"Mm?"

"Would you... Would you come with me?"

"I'm sorry?"

"I told father about you, how you're in the same boarding house as me, and he says he very much likes what you write and he asked me if I'd ask you if you want to pop by. And I said I would."

Mr Thark was frankly astonished. "Good heavens," he said. "A fan?"

"Oh, yes."

"How very blush-making. Is he a literary man?"

"He's an electrician."

"Oh, yes, you told me before, didn't you? But what I mean is, does he have books?"

"Only a little shelf."

He stood up. "Well then, I'd better come along, hadn't I?"

He nipped back up to his room to get his tweed jacket, and just as nimbly nipped down again. "Off we go," he said cheerfully.

9

It was a bright spring day, and Jenny's step was light as they walked down the street. "Isn't it lovely?" she said.

Mr Thark was determined to be contrary. "Yellow light, brisk breeze and a faint moisture. They've been on this setting nearly a week."

Jenny looked at him. "Don't you like it?"

"Maybe it's because I remember other times. A couple of days without a variation sends me absolutely nuts."

"Oh dear. Well, they'll probably be changing it tomorrow night."

"That's something to look forward to, I suppose. Where does your father live?"

"Oh, it's not far. Just down here."

They took a left turn along a small street fringed on both sides by neatly-built terraced houses in the old style. Jenny led Mr Thark to a house two-thirds along the left side. She went in without knocking.

"Hello, dad!" she called out. "It's only me and I've brought Mr Thark!"

"I'm in the kitchen," a voice came back.

Mr Threadneedle was filling a kettle as they entered the narrow kitchen area. "Tea, Mr Thark?" he asked, and Mr Thark nodded.

Jenny's father was a short, stocky man in his late fifties with a rosy, childlike face and sparse but unruly greying hair. He added extra water, stuck the whistle over the nozzle and parked it on the hob. Then, with a quizzical expression, he turned to Mr Thark and held out a hand. "Nice to meet you." And then, to Jenny: "So, how was school?"

Jenny related to him her adventures, first in the kitchen and then, the tea made, in the living room. It was a cramped little space, every surface covered with random clutter, the inevitable King's portrait sitting dusty and unloved amongst pens, pencils, scissors, and slide-rules.

When Jenny retold the incident of Miss Jones's arrest, Mr Threadneedle gave her a look which Mr Thark was puzzled to interpret.

"You won't do anything daft now, Jenny, will you?" said Mr Threadneedle. Jenny smiled at him and the conversation moved on.

Later, as Mr Thark's eye roved the room, it fell on a short row of paperbacks on a shelf in the corner. His face lit up.

"Your daughter told me you had books. I hope you don't mind if I have a look?"

"Why should I mind?" said Mr Threadneedle. "Go ahead, they're nothing special."

Mr Thark idly wandered over to the shelf while father and daughter continued to talk.

"Well, how are you doing, dad? Are they keeping you busy?"

"Oh, aye. The wiring up at the Palace is a right bodge-up. That'll keep us busy for a while yet in itself, never mind all the rest that needs fixing."

Mr Thark asked: "Is the wiring not good, then? I'd have thought..."

"You're better off not knowing," said Mr Threadneedle. "It'd only scare you."

"Really?"

Mr Threadneedle gestured vaguely. "Oh, you mustn't mind me, I like a good grumble sometimes. But look, Mr Thark–"

"Please – call me Desmond."

Mr Threadneedle's face broke into a smile. "Well, that's very nice of you, and you must call me Jack, if you will."

"Jack. Of course."

"But I was just saying, it's daft you being here and me talking about wiring when all I want to do is ask you about your work."

"Oh, lord! Work? I don't work, I write – I just get paid to enjoy myself."

"Me, I wouldn't know one end of the pen from the other. You know I read your column every week, religiously."

Mr Thark grew visibly embarrassed. "Now, really, really, I..."

"But then," Mr Threadneedle went on, "you don't need me to tell you they're not a patch on the ones you used to do in the old days."

"Ah! Now we come to it."

"Oh, I know it's not your fault, and don't think I'm criticising. You're making bricks without straw, aren't you, and it's amazing what you do

11

with what you've got. But you see I remember the old times before we came here."

Mr Thark looked over at the old man: yes, in his mind he saw Mr Threadneedle as old, even though, come to think of it, Mr Thark was surely the older of the two... and he saw that, bold though his words had been, Mr Threadneedle was not quite sure he had said the right thing. So Mr Thark paused, then slowly lifted his teacup and said, "I'll drink to that," and Mr Threadneedle grinned in relief.

Jenny excused herself to the bathroom, and the two men were left together. They were silent for a minute, Mr Threadneedle sipping his tea and glancing at Mr Thark over the lip of the cup as he drank.

"Jenny's a good lass," he said.

"I'm sure she is," said Mr Thark.

"I've brought her up as best I can. It's not been easy. But there's no point filling her with ideas that are no use to her, is there?"

"I suppose not," said Mr Thark, slightly puzzled.

"You're a friend of hers?"

"We live in the same lodgings. I like her."

"In some ways she's very trusting. She's loyal. I mean she stands up for the anthem and all that. And she means it too. I reckon it doesn't do for a person to be asking too many questions round here, and that's how she's been raised."

Mr Thark said: "What are you trying to say?"

Mr Threadneedle sighed. "I'm sure you're a very decent and respectable man, Mr Thark, Desmond. Only, I've read your stuff so I reckon I know a bit about you."

"Oh dear. You mustn't believe all you read. Especially the things I write. I've been seen to and everything."

"Yes, well. All I'm saying is, where Jenny's concerned, no funny business."

Mr Thark was taken aback. "No thought could be further from my mind."

12

Mr Threadneedle looked at him for a while. "Good," he said. "It had better not be."

A minute afterwards, Jenny came back down the stairs.

Later, as Mr Threadneedle's visitors were preparing to leave, he said to Mr Thark, "Thank you for coming. I know it's daft, but it means a lot." Mr Thark made a deprecating gesture, but he went on: "I saw you looking at some of my books. Take a couple if you want."

"Oh, I couldn't possibly," said Mr Thark, moving swiftly towards the shelves.

"I never look at them anyway. They're only cluttering up the house."

Mr Thark deftly selected three books, and almost before Jenny knew it, she and Mr Thark were out of the house and heading back to Mrs Cardigan's. The books were concealed in the pockets of his tweed jacket and a satisfied smile was on his face. Jenny glanced at him uncertainly but said nothing.

They let themselves into the lodging house and were standing in the hallway when Jenny at last spoke. "Mr Thark."

"Mm?"

"Why did you come?"

"Why, to see your father, of course."

"So it wasn't... to see his books?"

Mr Thark smiled. "Oh, bless your heart. That was part of it, of course. One doesn't pass up chances. But it was a real pleasure to meet your father. And after all, you did ask me to come along."

"Yes. Yes, I did. Forgive me, of course you're right."

"Thank you for inviting me," said Mr Thark, smiling his most charming smile. "It was a delight."

He started to ascend the stairs; then paused and turned, patting his jacket's breast pocket. "Besides," he added, "your father really does have *exceptional* taste in books."

CHAPTER THREE: The Library of Mr Thark

THAT AFTERNOON, QUITE SUDDENLY AND unexpectedly, the weather changed. The clear yellow light was gone; the air darkened, and in the next moment large round drops of water were floating down, drenching the Saturday shoppers.

Mr Thark hurried back into the lodging house and stood cursing in the hallway, his tweeds visibly soaked and his sparse hair plastered to his scalp.

Jenny popped her head round the doorway of the communal living room.

"Oh, hello," she said.

"Blasted rain," said Mr Thark.

"I thought you wanted a change in the weather?" Jenny asked. Mr Thark did not respond, but merely stomped upstairs to his room, where there was a towel and a change of clothes.

Ten minutes later, he came into the living room, where Jenny was reading Mr Thark's column in the *Gazette*.

> *It will be recalled that last week I had the honour of attending a lecture by HRH Prince Arthur Billikins at the Municipal Hall on the subject of Churchill and the Spirit of England.*
>
> *Well, this week I had the further good fortune of being invited to attend a lecture by HRH Prince Osric Beaufont at the same place, on the subject of Drake and the Spirit of England.*

While I cannot here do justice to the many piquant observations which flowed from His Royal Highness's facile lips it is sufficient to say that they were entirely characteristic and inimitable.

It was altogether a most magnificent occasion graced by the haute monde in its finest fig.

Amongst those present were: Lord Percival Patterson Mayor of High Hants with Lady Tilda Patterson, Sir Geraint and Lady Maud Hughes, the Datchet of Datchet, Mr and Mrs Harry Garner, and Mr Cuthbert Smythe.

Amongst those who stayed away were: Ms Glenda McHaggis, Mr Inigo Fotheringay-Trouser, the Mungo McMiffie of Muck, Lady Cecilia Throbbing, Sir Grassington Gorse of Thrope with Miss Drusilla Flange and Ponto, Mystico Magick (the Great), the Hon. Derek "Dangerstoat" Ottersniffer the Third, Dr Melody Duck, Barnaby Farnaby, Kimberley Camberley, Dick Flushing, and Sid Conk for the drains.

Afterwards we departed, having endured a most interesting talk.

We understand that next week HRH Prince Jimmy Vosper will be persuaded to dilate upon that (if possible) still more fascinating topic, Shakespeare and the Spirit of England.

God Save The King!

Mr Thark, dressed in green corduroys and a dark jumper with an old shirt underneath, and with his hair still wild from a brisk towelling, was calmer now, and even smiled at Jenny before seating himself in the chair opposite.

She glanced up at him. "Your column."

"Yes?"

"It's not my kind of thing. But I can see it must be quite funny."

"Why, thank you," he said drily.

He stood up and went to the window.

"It's absurd," he said. "Saturday afternoon! What are they thinking of?"

Jenny looked up again, but said nothing.

At length, Mr Thark turned around and said, "Look here, I feel I owe you an explanation."

"Do you?"

"I mean, about the books. Because the truth is I haven't been straight with you. No, that's not quite right; nothing I have told you was untrue. But..."

Mr Thark paused, embarrassed. Jenny was staring at him, not speaking. He came back to his chair and sat down, and, with an effort, tried again.

"You have to understand. When I... when we came here, we had to leave behind so much. Do you remember that? You must have been born on Earth, yes?"

"Yes," said Jenny quietly.

"But maybe you don't remember much about it. We were given an allowance for luggage, but so pitifully small... Most of us only brought a handful of books with us, six or seven... We didn't *think*. Well, I'm a writer so I was extravagant; I brought twelve. I even thought I took care in my selection. What a fool I was! I can't even bear to look at most of them anymore. Has your father ever talked to you about that time?"

"Not much."

"Maybe it's better that way. Well, when we got here the blinding fact struck us quite quickly... What we had with us was literally all we were ever going to get. If no one had brought... well, let's say *Love in a Cold Climate* or *A Handful of Dust*... then the fact is we wouldn't be reading them ever again."

"Sorry, what were those titles again?"

"*Love in a Cold Climate* and *A Handful of Dust*."

"I've never heard of them."

"Yes, exactly. Well, once I was here, I looked at what I had brought... and you know, there were only about three or four I could even bear to open. I mean, Thackeray? And of those twelve, there's only one that I really treasure." He rested his hand on the breast of his tweed jacket, which held a slight oblong bulge. "I keep it with me always."

"I see."

16

"I wonder if you do. If this is all you have ever known... How many books have you read?"

"Oh, Mr Thark, what a question! Books are my life. I've read so much... the whole of the King's Library."

"And your father's books too?"

"Only one or two. He said I was better off not reading them as they're not on the list."

"Quite. So in total, how many would you say? Twenty? Twenty-five?"

"Yes, about that."

Mr Thark sighed. "Well, Miss Threadneedle, back home, on Earth I mean, in London, I owned over three thousand books. Yes, it's true. And I don't know how many books were published every year, an unimaginable number. The journey I took to High Hants was a journey from feast to famine. To me, and to people like me, it became a matter of urgency to seek out from each other whatever crumbs we had brought. So you see, whenever there's a chance to get your hands on a title that you thought was gone for ever, well, you don't pass it up."

He had lowered his voice through the course of his speech, and now it was a hoarse croak, and they bent towards each other in their chairs. If he was going to talk about these things, and now that he had started he could not see how he could stop, then he should at least be sure that he wouldn't be overheard.

"And that, more or less," he rasped, "is how the Book Club started."

"The... Book Club?"

"Yes. The Book Club. Not an official gathering, of course. Miss Threadneedle, please promise me. Don't say anything about this to anyone. Not Mrs Cardigan, not your father, no one at your school, nobody. Do you promise?"

Jenny stared at him. Her eyes were a little frightened. "I promise."

"Good. So I can proceed. Miss Threadneedle, let me tell you how it works. Do you know the first rule of Book Club?"

"No. How should I?"

"The first rule of Book Club is... bring a book." He paused. Jenny looked at him. Mr Thark sighed. "Oh, never mind. Moving on. We simply visit each other and, well, exchange books. Simple, isn't it? If anyone asks, we're just meeting to play chess or bridge. But the books we bring are not the same as the books we take away. That's all. What possible harm could there be in such an innocent occupation?"

"None, indeed," Jenny said pensively. "But I don't quite understand."

"What don't you understand?"

"Well, what's wrong with the King's Library? It has all the literature anyone could need. *The Golden Treasury, Pride and Prejudice, Tales from Shakespeare...*"

Mr Thark sat back in his chair as if Jenny had slapped him. Then his expression changed, and he regarded her with wondering eyes. At last he spoke. "I see you don't understand me at all. I wonder, when you read, what do you think you are experiencing? Miss Threadneedle, I must tell you something and perhaps I should ask you to keep this as a great secret as well. Will you?"

"I don't know... Yes. Yes, I will. But Mr Thark, whatever can you be wanting to say?"

"Just this." He leant in again, beckoned her closer, and said:

"*There is never enough literature.*"

CHAPTER FOUR: Ticket to Ride

TEN MINUTES LATER, JENNY WAS in Mr Thark's flat. His desk, which was covered with papers and upon which there sat an old mug filled to bursting with an arsenal of pencils, stood by the window. Nearer the door, there was a tatty but comfortable armchair in green cloth, and by the side of this there was a table bearing a used teacup and saucer, a picture of the King, his face turned a little to one side, and a well-used copy of *The Best of Beachcomber*. The door to the bedroom was closed. In order to allow Jenny use of the armchair, Mr Thark had chosen to seat himself in a wooden work chair at the desk. However, Jenny was standing by his bookshelf, scanning the titles and listening to him as he continued to talk.

"Yes," he said, "over the years I have managed to increase my library considerably. Friends pass on; some swaps became permanent. I now have almost seventy books. I think that may be a record. Difficult to be sure in the circumstances. The only problem is that one must be so careful about telling anyone at all. Of course, you understand."

Jenny's expression did not wholly bear out this assumption, but Mr Thark proceeded, apparently without noticing.

"I've added your father's books to the shelf. Look. *The Prime of Miss Jean Brodie, Funeral in Berlin,* and *Blott on the Landscape*. Oh, there is such an ache in my heart just to see the titles. You know? I thought they were gone forever."

"Mm," said Jenny.

19

Mr Thark paused and looked at her. "You don't understand. How could you? You don't remember what it was like. Well, well. Your father would know."

"Yes, probably," said Jenny.

There was a pause. Jenny turned away from the shelf and walked to the window. Outside, the rain continued to splash onto the pavements in big, lazy drops. She sighed.

"Do you want to borrow a book?" Mr Thark asked.

Jenny stared unseeingly out of the window. "I don't think I should be here," she said.

"There's nothing to be afraid of. But if you're uncomfortable, if you want to go, please, I won't stop you."

Jenny shook her head impatiently. "It's not that. It's just... oh, I don't know. This is all so strange."

"What is?"

"What you are telling me."

Jenny had wandered away from the window, and now she sat in the armchair, a bewildered look on her face.

When Mr Thark spoke again, he did so carefully and slowly, as if stepping through a minefield. "Your father didn't talk to you much about life on Earth. Did he, did he ever talk about, well, freedom of speech?"

Jenny looked directly at him with her big blue eyes. "All speech is free, isn't it?"

Mr Thark gave a quick bark of laughter. "Your Miss Jones did not find it so."

"Oh, but that was quite different. *Quite* different. That was a matter of public order and, and obscenity."

"Indeed, indeed. And what about these books here on my shelf?"

"Well, they're not banned. Anyone can read them. Can't they?"

"And yet you are uncomfortable?"

"Maybe I am. You see, Mr Thark, and you mustn't think I am criticising you..."

"Please do."

"But I'm *not*. It just seems to me... maybe I'm wrong, but... just because people brought these books here and they are allowed to keep them on their shelves and to read them... isn't that different from now, well, seeking them out deliberately to be read as if they were somehow better and preferable to the books of the King's Library?"

"Yes. It is very different. You're right. But let me tell you something. On Earth, in England, where we came from, intellectual liberty was paramount... or at any rate some kind of lip service was paid to it. Being able to read anything one wanted was the measure of freedom."

"As it is here."

"Oh, absolutely. But the difference is that back on Earth not only could one do it, but one did. There was no King's Library of officially sanctioned books. You could read the foulest, most subversive nonsense, the cheapest, most illiterate trash, and no one could touch you for it."

"But why would you want to, if it was only trash and nonsense?"

"How would you know if it was trash and nonsense, if you didn't read it?"

Jenny's eyes strayed back to the bookshelf, as Mr Thark saw at once.

"Please," he said, "do take one. I can assure there is nothing so very bad there."

But still she hesitated. "If there's nothing wrong with them, why don't you want me to mention them to anyone?"

He leaned forward and lowered his voice. "We live in a place where even that which is not forbidden can get you arrested."

"I don't understand that."

"Neither do I. All the same, it is true. Listen. There was a member of the Book Club, a sweet, gentle man. Bernie Barker. You would have liked him. Well, five years ago, he disappeared. One day he was there, nursing his collection of Wodehouse and Jerome K. Jerome and, what was it, Miles Kington? What could be less dangerous? And the next, he was gone, and his landlady would not speak of it. He was simply erased.

21

So you see. Maybe there is freedom of speech. But only as long as it is the right kind of speech."

They looked for a long time at each other in silence. In that moment, something seemed to have happened, but they did not know what. It was something not expressed, and perhaps inexpressible; a bond seemed to have been forged.

Mr Thark stood up and looked out of the window at the rain and looked at the books on his shelf and picked a pen out of the mug on his desk and put in back again and sat down in exactly the same position as he had been a minute before.

"I want to tell you a story, Miss Threadneedle. I hope you don't mind. It's a true story; it's the story of what happened to me twenty years ago, and how it is that I came here.

"In those days, I lived in Houndsditch, in London. I was a columnist on the *Daily Record*. I wasn't like Tom Tattle in those days, trying to wring laughs out of, you know, funny names or speaking with a lisp, and always finishing with 'God Save the King'. No. I was permitted to do the job properly. I could say anything I liked, and I mean anything. But especially, and I want you to note this, especially the things that people didn't want me to say. You will think I am just another old man boasting of his triumphs, and of course I am. But all the same, let me tell you this. I was the best of the bunch. Yes, I was. There was a whole generation of us, and I was the one they feared and hated because I was the one who did it *right*. Look on the shelf. Yes, there."

Jenny picked out the book, an almost-pristine paperback, and looked at it. "*Mad, Quite Mad* by Desmond Thark," she read. "Oh, I'm sorry, I didn't notice the name before. It's yours?"

"Of course. You think I would come here without one of my own books? The best of the *Mad World, My Masters* column. Naturally, most of it won't make much sense to you. It's all about the passing controversies of the day, and yesterday's jokes are today's arsewipes, pardon my French. But it may give you some idea, all the same."

Jenny opened the book at random. She saw a passage explaining that the true oppressed minority was the heterosexual white male. She turned to another page. It was all about some things called "libtards" and she did not understand it at all, though a scent of acrid bitterness leapt from the page. She closed the book.

"I see," she said, not seeing.

"I'm very proud of those pieces," Mr Thark said, leaning back in his chair and closing his eyes with a complacent smile. "If I have a masterpiece, it is that book. But that's not the point. I only showed you it so you would understand. There were a few of us, three or four, writing in that line. There was me, and there was Giles Chalfont, and Jiminy Jobson, and... oh, what was his name? Well, anyway, as I said there were a few of us.

"You have to understand that the *Record*, and a lot of the other papers, the *Sentinel*, the *Telegram*, the *Posthorn* which was Giles's billet... we were all owned by the same man, Sir Richmond Rotherham. Do you remember him?"

Jenny shook her head.

"No, maybe not. He died not long after he came here. He was famous in his day, a kind of god to some of us... a capricious god and more than slightly mad. He had enthusiasms, you see, and when he had them we all had to have them. For instance, I remember when... well, that doesn't matter. The point is, it was about this time that the Lunar Project went public, and... Perhaps I need to explain about that.

"At that time, we had a stable, prosperous society, we were in the midst of plenty. Everything was fine. Well, it wasn't, of course, but we thought it was. And anyway, that's how I made my living, telling people that everything was all right, and that nothing had to change. The fact that I sincerely believed it, helped too.

"So when the Project was first mooted by this group of... what would you call them? Men, Englishmen, having done well with their investments, now at their leisure to survey the world and put it to rights... when they put forward this project of theirs to set up a colony on the

23

Moon and make of it a little England... all we could do was laugh. We wrote columns laying into the whole scheme, reducing it to rubble with the force of our ridicule. We called it the Loony Project, I remember.

"And that was all fine and dandy until we all got the memo... It seemed Sir Richmond had been looking into the Project and he was now one of its firmest advocates, and we were all instructed to boost it as much as we jolly well could in our respective papers.

"Well, at first I tried maintaining a dignified silence on the whole subject, but then I was told in no uncertain terms that wasn't enough. So I did it. I wrote about it. But I wasn't happy.

"My writing depends on sincerity; I have to feel it in my heart. There is always a part of me that can argue for a contrary opinion, of course; that's part of the arsenal; and I can unleash it when necessary. But it was hard. Especially hard because I was directly contradicting all the things I had been saying about the damn thing two weeks before. Usually I don't mind what people say about me. Water off a duck's back. But this was humiliating. Nevertheless, it had to be done, so I did it, and I thought that was that.

"But I was wrong. Because it was only a couple of weeks later that the Grand Raffle was announced.

"By this time, the Lunar Project was already underway. It was actually quite far advanced, though they'd managed to keep it under wraps somehow. Ships had been sent out to establish the site and lay the groundwork. And the structure had been set up, and the buildings were being built. It was suddenly clear the damn thing was actually going to happen. These, these moneyed idiots really were going to leave the planet for a better life on the Moon in some farcical simulacrum of an imagined past. Now don't get me wrong," (Mr Thark raised his voice a little), "that's what I thought then, it's not what I think now, *no*, by no means. But they wanted people to go. Not just the super-wealthy, but the workers who would maintain it in good working order, and the middling sort too, the kind of people that provide stability and prevent revolution. People like us. Sir Richmond was going, and he wanted a selection of the best and brightest from his newspapers to go with him. So we happy few were entered in the Raffle, and we had no choice, we couldn't refuse it. If we won, we had to go, and no excuses. No empty seats allowed on that voyage out.

"I remember the night before the Grand Draw. We were all getting a bit hysterical. I was good friends with Giles Chalfont, and he came round to my place with a crate of red and we got thoroughly plastered and laughed at it all and laughed. It was laughter in the shadow of the gallows. He said to me: 'What are you worried about, Desmondo? It's your bloody wet dream isn't it, England for the English?' And I denied it and said he was mixing me up with himself.

"Next day, we all had hangovers, every man jack of us. We staggered into work and the Raffle took place in the foyer of Rotherich House. The Grand Fromage was there in person to cast his baleful eye over us all as the pink slips were pulled and make sure none of us snuck off. I felt sick, Miss Threadneedle, thoroughly sick. My heart beat so hard it nearly broke. Every number they called was another nail in my coffin. But then, almost all the numbers had been called and they hadn't called mine. I didn't feel relieved. I knew they were only saving me up for last. And so the final number came, and I couldn't believe it, I felt as if I would pass out from the relief, because it was not mine. But then I heard a cry that could not be suppressed somewhere to my left, and I saw Giles staring at me with such a look as I have never seen. It was of course his number.

"That night, he told me quite frankly, 'I can't do it, Desmondo. I simply can't. It's awful. You can't expect me actually to go off like Flash Bloody Gordon into the deep blue and float about on another world. Old boy, it's not on and we all know it's not.'

"It took another year, I think, before the ships started going out in earnest, bearing the people who would set up house in High Hants, as they had now decided to call the place. I think Giles had a sort of hope that it would never really come to pass in the end. Maybe he was planning to drink himself to death before it happened, but that's difficult to tell because it would not have involved any great change to his lifestyle.

"As I say, he couldn't back out. His seat on the ship out had to be filled. There simply wasn't any other option.

"In the meantime, I myself was doing very nicely, thank you. I seemed to have struck a perfect seam in my talent. It was one last song before the end came. That was the summer when the future at last became clear. The sun burned hot. The droughts struck. The air became thin. We gasped for breath. People died. We drove our cars to escape into our own little air-conditioned bubble, and as we drove the fumes belched into the ever hotter air. The trees were burning. We knew we were doomed, it was all coming to an end, though not everyone could quite bear to say it. And all at once I was finding it harder and harder to maintain that careless gaiety in my columns which was their whole point and virtue. I lay awake at night in an oppressive terror. I could see no way out.

"Or, rather, I could see one way out. But it wasn't mine, it was Giles's.

"I went to see him once. He couldn't write any more. The *Posthorn* had to pension him off in the end, it was pitiful. He was just sitting at home knocking back endless supplies of Tesco plonk watching *Supermarket Sweep* or whatever it was. He knew at once what was in my mind. Either it was telepathy between libertarians, or he could tell from my face. 'Take it,' he said. 'Take that bloody ticket, do me a favour.' I told him, 'It won't work, they want you,' but he came back saying, 'Do you think they can tell the difference between us? We're just spewing out the same filthy stuff, you and me and you again.'

"Well, I laughed him off and I... no, I can't say I thought no more of it, because I did. I thought more of it every day. But I never really believed it would happen. Until, that is, that day, the day before. I got a phone call from Susan, his ex. She said Giles was paralytic and refusing to come out of the toilet. I went round and I tried to talk to him. He was out of control, right up to the moment he passed out. It was obvious he wasn't going anywhere the next day, never mind the Moon. Then

Susan went to his desk and opened the top drawer and handed me the ticket.

"And that was it. I took the ticket, I went home, I packed my bags. I agonised over my twelve books, though I might as well have spared myself the trouble. Next day, I went to the launch site, which was somewhere in Oxfordshire. I went through Security like a dream. They barely looked at the ticket, which of course had the wrong name on it. Giles was right, damn him. They couldn't bloody tell us apart. They wanted a truth-telling journalist of a certain sort, and they got him. When I was standing in that bizarre line of pale and loitering journalists... of course paleness was one of the criteria but we were all especially pale that day... the great ship loomed above us and I felt a sudden desire to laugh. It was all so grotesquely ridiculous. And yet, in the end it was just prosaic. We were guided on, we were told how to strap ourselves in, and, after the most hellishly awful hour in my entire life, we were on our way... here."

Mr Thark stopped talking. He slumped back in his chair, spent, and for a long time there was silence.

"My father," said Jenny, "came here because he was needed. He's an electrician – but you know that. He tried to persuade Mum to come too, but she said no."

Mr Thark looked at her in surprise. "Your mother?"

"Yes. Didn't you wonder about her? She said she couldn't leave home. She said it would be like treachery when she was needed most."

"Why? Was she... some kind of activist?"

"No, I don't think so. I don't know what she meant, exactly. Of course I'm only going by what Dad told me once. I don't remember Mum at all, myself."

Jenny stood up.

"Thank you for talking to me. I enjoyed it. I think I should be going now. The rain has stopped and I would like to take a walk before curfew."

27

Mr Thark smiled. "I should be thanking you. I needed to get it all out, even if you didn't need to hear it. Please take a book, it's the least I can do."

"Oh, I couldn't possibly..."

"Please." Mr Thark went over to the shelf and, after a moment's pause, selected a volume. "There. Jane Austen. No one could possibly object."

Jenny left Mr Thark's room before looking at it. Then, glancing down at as she stood on the dark staircase, she smiled.

It was *Persuasion*.

CHAPTER FIVE: Stone Walls Do Not a Prison Make

NEXT MORNING, MRS CARDIGAN AND her lodgers, dressed in their Sunday best, paraded down the road and attended the service at the Church of St Joseph of Arimathea.

The Vicar, the Reverend Anselm Headlong, gave a long sermon on Brotherly Love, and the congregation sang, "I Vow to Thee, My Country", while Mr Thark mouthed the words as usual and Jenny sang in a clear voice.

After they had returned home, Jenny went up to her room to change. She sat on her bed for a long time, thinking.

She stood up, completed her toilet, selected a hat, put on her weighted shoes, slipped on her coat, and descended the stairs once more. "I'm just going out for a while," she told Mrs Cardigan. "I should be back by three."

Once in the street, she turned to the right, which led away from the centre of the town. She passed down residential roads, quite empty and without litter. It was as if faces peered out through the curtains at her, though she tried to believe this only was her imagination.

And now she was approaching the city's edge, where the great enclosing dome descended in front of her and became solid. The street down which she walked opened out onto a plaza. Opposite her, on the other side of the square, was the infinite wall that was the end of High Hants, and in its blank face there was just one small door, which she knew to be the entrance to the Marshalsea Prison.

29

She walked up to the door and rapped on it as confidently as she could pretend.

The door opened.

"Yes?" said a voice in the darkness.

"I, um, I would like to see Miss Jones, please."

"Miss who?"

"Jones."

"First name?"

"I don't know."

There was a pause.

"You're not making it easy, are you?" said the voice.

"I suppose not," said Jenny. "She was arrested on Monday."

"I'll ask."

The door was slammed shut, and Jenny waited outside. After six minutes, the door opened again. "Come in."

Jenny was led down a grubby corridor into a waiting area. There was one other person there, seated on a hard wooden chair. Jenny seated herself three seats down from her.

Fifteen minutes later, the other person was called through.

After a further ten minutes, the man came back in and beckoned to her. Jenny followed him into a large room with twenty bare tables in it, arranged geometrically, every table having a hard chair on each side of it. The King's picture on the wall was unusually large and oppressive. Miss Jones was seated at a table on the other side of the room. The man said to Jenny, "Keep your hands on the table. Don't touch. You've got five minutes." Jenny walked over to the table and sat down.

"You shouldn't be here," said Miss Jones.

"How are you?" Jenny asked.

Miss Jones looked at her. "Why have you come?" she asked.

"I wanted to see you."

"Please. I appreciate your coming but you should go."

"But I'm here now. Can't we talk?"

Miss Jones did not reply for a minute. Then she said: "It's not safe for you here. Don't you know that?"

"Are they treating you well?"

"Oh, yes, yes, as far as that goes. You know of course that I'm going to die."

"Don't say that."

"I must. That's how it is. It's all arranged. They'll sedate me and put me out of the airlock. I knew it when I did it, and they will. Don't worry about me. I planned it this way."

"But why?"

Miss Jones sighed. "Don't ask. You're making it worse. Now I insist. For your own good. Please go."

"What do you mean?"

Miss Jones did not reply.

"What do you mean? Why won't you answer me?"

Jenny asked question upon question, but she saw that Miss Jones had decided not to answer, and she stood up.

"Thank you for seeing me," she said. "I don't understand, I don't understand anything. But... well, I hope it all turns out all right for you."

Miss Jones smiled thinly, but spoke no more.

Jenny put up her hand in farewell and turned and left.

The man guided her out of the building. She turned her back on the prison and returned the way she had come, arriving back at the lodgings in time to sit down to Sunday lunch (nut roast) with Mr Thark and the Ogilvys. The radio was tuned to *Family Favourites*.

Jenny was quiet all through the meal; indeed, there was almost no conversation at all. Afterwards, she was about to enter her flat when Mr Thark's head appeared over the banister above her, and he called down the stairs.

"Oh, Miss Threadneedle, wait a minute, will you?" he said. His head disappeared, reappearing a minute later, attached to his body, as he hurried downstairs to meet her on the landing.

31

"I just thought you might want this," he said, handing her a small slip of card. "It was in one of the books from your father's shelf, but I only noticed it before lunch today."

Jenny looked at it. It was a strip of two identical photographs, head and shoulder shots of a young woman with dark hair, seated in front of a white screen. The top of the strip was cut at a very slight angle, as if there had originally been more photos. The woman had a broad, slightly square face, deep blue eyes and a mouth which was not smiling and yet not quite unsmiling.

"Oh," said Jenny. "Thank you."

"Is it...?" said Mr Thark.

"Yes," said Jenny. "That's my mother."

She was about to turn and go into her room, when she paused for a moment and, not turning her face to him, added: "Thank you."

"My pleasure," said Mr Thark.

That night, Jenny lay awake, listening to the world outside her window. The great slats scraped and clanked as they adjusted; tomorrow slightly more light would filter through the dome and there would be a little more spring in the air. Perhaps there would be a different loop of birdsong, too.

She was finding it difficult to sleep. Change was about, and it was not just the promise of spring. For the first time in a long while, she felt the tightness of the straps. She was not an introspective kind of person, and as a rule she did not query the way things were. But then and there she could sense the shape of the questions that she could not quite frame. It was disquieting.

She listened out for the curfew wagon. It was late.

She could almost feel the dome of High Hants pressing down on her, and beyond it, the unimaginable void of the Moon's surface and the stars and of that other place.

The low rumble came as the wagon crawled down the street. It stopped and there was a brief scuffle. A voice was abruptly cut short and the van's door was slammed. After a pause, the van proceeded again, fading into the distance.

And again she felt it: somewhere out there, through the vacuum of space, casting its strange reflected glow onto the Moon, unseen by anyone, the great milky globe of the Earth; the place she was born.

CHAPTER SIX: The Name of the Law

JENNY HAD ONLY BEEN TEACHING at the school a week, but already it felt was as if she had been there forever. That Monday, she went in at seven-thirty, prepared the board, and welcomed the children like lifelong friends as they entered.

In fact, the stranger arrived during the morning assembly, though Jenny, seated at the end of her class's row and facing forwards, did not see him as he stood silently at the back of the hall. Mr Jorrocks flickered a puzzled glance at him, which Jenny did not notice.

It was only as the children were filing out of the hall afterwards that the man made himself known to her, stepping in front of her and removing his hat with a gesture that could have been courteous but which seemed, from this tall, lean figure with the clipped brown moustache and the paper-white face, somehow sinister and even threatening.

"Miss Threadneedle?" he said.

"Yes?"

"I wonder if I could have a word."

"Well, be quick, I have a class."

The man smiled bleakly. "I don't think you understand."

"I don't think I do."

"This is not something we can rush."

"I'm sorry?"

By now, the children had streamed into their classes, and Jenny became aware of the emptiness of the corridor.

"Who are you, did you say?" she said.

"Oh, but I didn't."

At this moment, Mr Jorrocks came bustling up.

"Miss Threadneedle, why aren't you in class?" he wheezed.

"I was just wondering the same thing, Headmaster. This gentleman was..."

"Permit me," the man said. He took a card out of the inner pocket of his jacket and showed it to Mr Jorrocks, whose eyes widened in shock.

"Oh," Mr Jorrocks said. "I'm sorry, I didn't realise..."

"Quite all right, Headmaster," the man said smoothly. "Now, I would just like to have a word with Miss Threadneedle, if I may. In private."

"Of course, of course," said Mr Jorrocks, suddenly obsequious to this strange man. "Perhaps my study would be most convenient?"

"By all means. If you would show me the way?"

Jenny puzzled over the change in Mr Jorrocks as they walked back down the corridor, across the assembly hall, and through the other side, to the headmaster's study. What was it that had passed across his face like a cloud? Was it fear?

Mr Jorrocks opened the door for them, and with a sickly smile said to the man: "Take as long as you need. Just let me know when you are done, please. I will be looking after Miss Threadneedle's class."

"Thank you, Headmaster," said Jenny. "I don't imagine we'll be long."

"Don't you?" said the man, shutting the door in the headmaster's face.

Jenny swallowed, and resolved to be as calm and confident as possible in the presence of this man, to whom she had taken as thorough a dislike as she had ever experienced in her life.

"Now," she said. "Who are you and what do you want?"

The man did not move. He stood with his back against the closed door and looked at Jenny unblinkingly.

"It's very simple, Miss Threadneedle. I only need to know one simple thing and then you can go."

Jenny considered sitting down in the visitor's chair, but decided it put her at too much of a disadvantage. She remained standing, a hand resting on the edge of the Headmaster's desk. There was a cane negligently thrown across the tabletop after its last use; she moved it gently away from her.

"Are you the police?" she asked.

"You're very clever," he said. "I can see that."

"I'm not answering any questions if I don't know who you are."

The man considered this. "Call me Goffin," he said.

"Is that your name?"

"It's what I'm called."

It occurred to Jenny that this was not quite the same thing, but decided on the whole not to press the matter.

"All right then. What do you want to know?"

Goffin smiled. "Why did you visit Miss Begonia Jones at the Marshalsea yesterday?"

Jenny could not help it; her head jerked up and she stared at him. "Begonia?"

"Don't evade the question."

"I wasn't, I was just... Well, all right. I went to see her because I wanted to know how she was."

"Why?"

"Why? Because I liked her. I still do. I wanted to know if she was all right."

"Is she an old friend of yours?"

"I only met her last Monday."

"So why would you care if she was well or ill? If you had only met her that day?"

"It doesn't take a year to know you like someone. It doesn't take an hour."

"And you were there when she was arrested, weren't you?"

"You know I was."

"So you know why she was arrested."

36

"Yes."

"And yet, knowing that, you still went to see her."

Jenny started to move away from the desk. She walked towards the window, which looked over the playground. It was empty, and it was almost shining with the strange grey light of a High Hants morning. Jenny turned away from the window, avoiding the eye of the King which glared at her from the adjacent wall, and looked over at Goffin.

"Is it illegal?"

"That was not my question."

"Because if it isn't illegal, I don't understand what concern it is of yours."

Goffin sighed. "I think, even now, you don't quite see the point. This is my job, Miss Threadneedle: investigating subversive elements. It's not up to me to prove anything. It's up to you to prove otherwise."

"Mr... Goffin. This is ridiculous. I've done nothing wrong. In fact, you've just confirmed as much. I've nothing more to say. And as I have already told you, I have a class to teach, so if you'll excuse me..."

Jenny walked to the door and stood before Goffin, waiting for him to move. He stared at her with those cold, lifeless eyes.

"I know you," he said between his clenched teeth.

"You don't," Jenny said.

"You pretend innocence, here in this school of yours. Good as gold, aren't you? But all the same, I know you. Bent as a nine bob note, that's you. Aren't you."

"Please move."

He paused, then with an insolent gesture took a step to one side.

"You're nothing but a piece of shit," he whispered.

Jenny opened the door.

"Goodbye, Mr Goffin."

"Till next time, Miss Threadneedle," he said with that smile of his. Jenny walked away without looking back.

It took her a while to recover from the interview. She could feel herself quivering all over, and she had to restrain the urge to shout at her innocent pupils. She knew she had to calm herself down, so she opened the book in front of her and read to them Wordsworth's "Daffodils." Afterwards, a dreamy silence fell over her and she was at peace again.

A hand shot up. "Miss? Miss?"

"Yes, Jeremy?"

"What's a daffodil?"

After school, when Jenny had tidied everything and was on her way back home, she was quite calm and while, of course, she had not forgotten that morning's encounter, it was already something that had been put to one side in her mind.

The street opened out onto Empire Road. Mrs Cardigan's boarding house stood on Empire Road almost opposite the street's mouth, slightly to its left. As she came to the end of the street, she anticipated nothing out of the ordinary, and indeed was scarcely paying any attention to her surroundings. She had barely had time to register, in a detached sort of way, that a police van was parked outside the house, when all at once a strong hand took her by the arm and pulled her into the doorway of Harrison's Boiled Sweets.

She wrested her arm free and turned indignantly towards her assailant, but the angry words on her lips died when she saw the man was Mr Thark, a serious and almost sickened expression on his face.

"In here," he hissed. "Don't speak. Grave matters are afoot."

The bell tinkled as they entered the shop.

CHAPTER SEVEN: Persons of Interest

"AFOOT?" SAID JENNY.

The shop was dark and badly lit; it was not immediately clear where they had precipitated themselves.

"Good afternoon," said a little old lady dressed in some dusty faded material which gave the impression of being on the verge of crumbling into dust, emerging from the darkness at the back of the shop. She smiled shyly at them from behind the counter. "May I assist you?"

Jenny looked around her. Yes, indeed, it was the sweet shop she had half-seen a hundred times as she passed that way, the great jars of brightly-coloured drops arrayed on shelves stretching to the ceiling, the smaller wrapped bags and twists arranged in rows at the counter, the tatty cardboard signs proclaiming "HUMBUGS 4 oz. / 2d." and the like, a scuffed and tatty English flag bearing the King's face pinned on the counter's front. She could not recall anyone ever entering the place, not even children coming home from school, and the place was empty now except for themselves.

"We're just looking, thank you," said Mr Thark, and the little old lady nodded as if to say, "I wish only to serve."

Mr Thark took Jenny by the arm again and guided her to a corner of the shop. "Yes," he hissed. "Afoot. Ay Eff Double Oh Tee. And I think you know very well what I am talking about."

A feeling of sick dread began to steal over Jenny, but she said nothing.

"It so happens," said Mr Thark in the same low, urgent tone, "that I was visiting a friend this afternoon. I was walking back when I saw the van in the street. I have been in that doorway for several centuries, watching them. They've been in my room. Yours too. Yours first, I think." Then he added: "They've taken my books."

Jenny gasped. "Oh no! Oh, I am sorry."

She looked into his face and she saw that he could not speak, so great was the anger that threatened to overwhelm him. It was terrible; it was awful; but she knew that she had to tell him what had happened.

"Mr Thark," she began. "I'm sorry. I mean that from the bottom of my heart. I can't believe that any action of mine could have caused this and I can assure you that nothing, nothing I have done is in any way wrong or even in the slightest degree improper. But yesterday afternoon I did visit Miss Jones in prison because I..."

"You did what?" Mr Thark's voice was low and strained but it had the force of a shout.

"I visited her in prison," Jenny said.

"But are you, don't you realise, why did you, I mean why would you, what?"

"Because I like her. And because I'm allowed to. They invited me in."

"Said the spider to the fly."

"Sorry?"

"Never mind. So what she have to say for herself?"

"She told me to go away."

"Of course she did. And then?"

"Then I went away. And then this morning..."

"There's more?"

"This morning a man came to see me at school. He asked me a lot of strange questions but of course I hadn't broken the rules and he knew it, and I sent him on his way and went back to my class."

Mr Thark turned his face away slightly and it was as if his mouth were chewing on something. She watched him silently. He turned back; his expression was quite calm.

"There's no point blaming anyone now. I'm older than you and unfortunately I know these people. They don't care about the rules. They are the rules. You visited this Miss Jones, this known subversive."

"Oh, but that's nonsense, she hasn't even been tried, how can..."

"This known subversive," Mr Thark repeated. "That makes you a subversive too. Can't you see how it works? If she were at large they would be following her. But she's in prison, so they follow her associates. You. And your associates too. That means me. Your father. Everyone in the house. The Ogilvys. Mrs Cardigan, for God's sake! We're all persons of interest. And now they've got my library, they know the kind of terrible, subversive literature I have been reading... *Catch-22, Decline and Fall,* Tom Sharpe... they'll have impounded your Jane Austen, you can be sure of that..."

His voice trailed off and he looked sharply over at the counter. It was empty. The door to the back room was ajar, and the two could hear, at the edge of hearing, a low mumble, followed by the click of a replaced receiver. The woman looked at them fearfully through the jamb of the door.

No words were needed. Mr Thark, Jenny close behind, hurried out of the shop and started walking briskly down the street, away from Empire Road and the police van. "Don't run," Mr Thark muttered. "Act normal."

But already they could hear voices behind them, and steps heading their way. They increased their pace, first to a faster walk, and then to a trot. Jenny's mind was racing. It was absurd, she had done nothing wrong, she had nothing to fear from the police, and yet at the same time she knew in her heart that she, they, had to escape.

But, all the same, how could they? Already the steps were closer. They could hear the men's voices shouting for them to stop. Jenny was not trained to run. As for Mr Thark, he was in no condition for such exertion, and was already wheezing. The race had only just started, but already it was as good as over.

But now she heard Mr Thark make a small noise of triumph. He took her by the hand and cried, "This way!"

All at once she was following him, without considering the wisdom of it, over to the other side of the street and into the cool darkness of the Church of St Joseph of Arimathea. He pushed the great door shut behind them with a deep boom.

They stood there for a moment, regaining their breath.

"But they know we're here," Jenny said.

"Of course they do," Mr Thark gasped. He held up a hand to allow him to recover his breath. "That's not the point. Haven't you heard of sanctuary?"

She nodded. "Oh yes. Of course. Does that still apply? It seems rather... historical."

Mr Thark grinned mirthlessly. "Maybe you're right. But it's worth a try, don't you think?"

At the same moment, the men outside started hammering on the door. "Come out!" a man shouted. "Come out in the name of the law!"

"They don't want to come in," Mr Thark whispered. "They're not sure!"

Jenny and Mr Thark walked down the nave of the church towards the chancel. The continued hammering on the door boomed round the high-vaulted building, which had been built in imitation of its stone cousins on Earth, only in concrete.

"Where are we going?" Jenny asked.

"Who cares? Away from them, anyway."

At this moment, a shadow stirred in the darkness and, to their heart-stopping dismay, a figure stepped out. "Who is that?" a mild voice asked.

"Oh, Reverend Headlong," Jenny cried in relief. "I'm so glad to see you!"

"Ah, Miss Threadneedle, isn't it? And Mr Thark too, I am blessed! How may I assist you?"

In response, Mr Thark gestured with his head towards the door. There had been a brief pause in the noise outside, but this now resumed.

42

Bang, bang, bang, bang – "Open up in the name of the law!" – Bang, bang, bang, bang – "We know you're in there!"

The Reverend cocked an inquiring eyebrow. "For you?"

Mr Thark nodded. "Some gentlemen that we don't want to meet just now."

"Well," said the Reverend thoughtfully, "we shall have to do something about that, won't we?" With a gesture of old-world apology, he excused himself and ambled down the nave towards the great double doors.

"What are you going to do?" Mr Thark called. The old vicar merely waved a hand as he continued towards the door.

"I'm sure he has some cunning strategy," Jenny said.

They watched him approach the doors as the hammering continued, then, during a brief pause in the racket, call out, "Just a minute, please," and turn the handle and pull the door open. Jenny saw him stand to one side and gesture towards herself and Mr Thark. The policemen stormed in.

She heard a muttered "Bugger!" next to her, and at once she and Mr Thark were running towards the door which stood ajar by the right-hand transept.

On the other side of the door they found a wide staircase leading upwards. "Of course," Mr Thark growled. "Frabjous day." They leapt up the stairs, hearing the shouts of the police behind them.

As they ran madly up the stairs in a square spiral, Jenny's mind raced. Of course they were in the church's clock tower. Of course they would end up on the platform at the top which afforded such an impressive view across the little world of High Hants. But what then? What hope was for them now? This surely was the last act of their brief drama.

So they ran higher and higher, round and round, till they were almost giddy and certainly light-headed.

And now they were standing on the platform, the carefully regulated breeze wafting across the town from the westward ventilators, the blue dome above them visibly false and gleaming, the town a hundred feet below them a circumscribed disc. They came to a stop, bewildered and hopeless.

"How childish it all is," Mr Thark sighed. "Well, Miss Threadneedle, this is it. Let us face our fate with dignity."

He turned to her with a grave face, and was surprised to see in her eye a sudden gleam and on her face a wild grin. "Sod that, as I think you would say," she cried. "Take off your shoes!"

"What?"

"Take off your shoes! Quick!"

Already she was unbuckling her shoes and slipping them off.

"Are you mad?" Mr Thark cried, even as, in automatic response to her command, he too started to unlace his footwear.

"Mr Thark," she laughed in response, as she stepped out of her second shoe and with a little hop was already nearly floating in the air, "have you really forgotten where we are? We are on the Moon!"

And Jenny grasped his hand and pulled him towards the edge of the parapet, and with a wild cry they both leapt over the edge into the light air above the crazy city.

CHAPTER EIGHT: With One Bound

AS HE AND JENNY, HAND in hand, floated down towards the street like dandelion seeds cast into the air by a sudden gust, Mr Thark found himself laughing madly. Why hadn't he thought of it himself? There they were, the inhabitants of High Hants, every one of them donning their weighted shoes every day to counteract the feeble gravity of their little world, and here he was, running around in flight from the police and never even giving a thought to the great heavy weights that he himself had strapped onto his feet, which held him down and made his own capture so inevitable. It took, he realised, someone who had lived in High Hants as a curious and inquisitive child testing the why and wherefore of everything, to know what really could be done when the crunch came. Why, he and Jenny were free! Surely no one could catch them now; their superpower had been unleashed. Mr Thark, the new Springheeled Jack, would evade capture at every crisis with this simple ruse, and Jenny too was forever liberated through the same stratagem. This, then, was the end of all their problems!

At this moment they bumped gently down on the pavement. They could hear the cries of the police behind them, tumbling through the church again and onto the street. The chase was afoot once more. Mr Thark pushed forward and was bouncing along in his stockinged feet before he knew it, Jenny keeping pace easily.

But within seconds his thoughts were taking a gloomier turn. This was no solution after all. No matter where they went, they were trapped. There was nowhere to escape *to*. And who would take them in? Every eye was in the service of the King. Even his buddies at the Book Club, would he trust them even as far as he could trust himself, which was no great distance? No, no, certainly not.

Of course (his thoughts continued as they sped round a corner and towards the parked electrician's van) the great thing was running away from rather than running to, and they were doing fine well on that front so far; but the question did have to be faced sometime: where to, where to?...

"In here!"

Quicker than he could think, he could see the van doors were open at the back and a hand was extended and grabbing them, guiding them in. The doors closed behind them swiftly but quietly, and the van was on its way before he could even find a seat.

He was looking round him and trying to work out what had just happened, registering Jenny who was sitting opposite him on a sort of hard banquette, as was he, he noticed, and casting his eye forward and back in the darkness of the van's rear area.

He saw, turning back in the passenger seat in front and grinning, a face he had seen before. It was Jenny's father, Jack. "That was close," Jack said.

Mr Thark found himself struggling to know what to say, so he said the first thing that he knew had to be expressed, which was, "Thank you."

"No trouble, no trouble at all," said Mr Threadneedle. Then, "Well, as a matter of fact, it was a *bit* of trouble. But it had to be done. How's it going, our lass?"

"Good, thanks, dad," said Jenny. "Thanks."

"But what happened?" said Mr Thark. "How did you..."

"How did I know? Well, the police tramping up the path in their big flat boots and banging on my door was the first clue," said Mr Threadneedle cheerfully. "I thought, 'What's our Jenny been getting up to now?' So after I'd sent them away with a flea in their ear, it was just a matter of working out how to get to you."

"A flea in their ear? How did you manage that?"

"Oh, I'm not as daft as I look," said Mr Threadneedle. "I can look after myself, don't you worry."

"But didn't they look round your house?"

"Of course."

"So what about your books?"

"What books? They didn't find no books."

Mr Threadneedle smiled at Mr Thark beatifically for a moment as the van, trundling along with a high electric whine, bumped over a pothole in the road.

"Where are we going, dad?" Jenny asked.

"Ah, well, I'm glad you asked me that. I've got a few ideas in my head. But we'll have to be heading somewhere else first, we've got a job on."

"A job?" Mr Thark asked.

"Aye, that's right, a job of work," said Mr Threadneedle. "What do you think I do all day? We got the call out half an hour ago, so they're expecting us. Best stay in the van for the moment. Oh, by the way, you'll be wanting to meet Frank. Frank, this is my daughter Jenny, and this is Mr Desmond Thark, one of our most respected writers."

"Charmed, I'm sure," said the driver of the van.

"He's the strong, silent type," said Mr Threadneedle.

"And, um, trustworthy?" Mr Thark asked in some embarrassment, knowing that Frank himself could hear the question but at the same time unable to avoid asking it.

"Frank? Don't be daft, Frank's all right. Aren't you, Frank?"

"That's right," said Frank.

"There you go."

Now they were slowing down. They bumped off the road onto a gentle downward ramp which took them out of the outdoor light and into an underground parking area. Long neon strips blinked at them harshly from the low concrete ceiling. They could hear the cold and desolate echo that is the mark of all such places. Frank selected a space by a far wall and, with some care, parked.

"Where are we?" Mr Thark asked, trying to peer out of the grimy back panel.

"Ah, now there's a question for you," said Mr Threadneedle. "You'll never guess."

CHAPTER NINE: Long Live the King

"The Palace?" Mr Thark cried. "We're in the Palace?"

"Underneath really," said Mr Threadneedle. "When you come to think of it, it's the safest place for you. Who'd think of looking here?"

"Hm," said Mr Thark.

"Cheer up, we won't be long," said Mr Threadneedle.

"How long?"

"Oh, not longer than an hour. Probably less. Don't fret, you'll be quite all right here." He made to open the door.

"Wait," said Mr Thark. "Where are we going after this? Where are you taking us?"

"Does it matter?"

"Of course it matters."

"Well," said Mr Threadneedle teasingly, "can't you guess, a smart man like you?"

Mr Thark made an impatient gesture, and Mr Threadneedle relented. "All right, all right, I'll tell you. What about the Ecosphere?"

"Ah," said Mr Thark. Why hadn't he thought of that? Of course, the moon base did not consist only of the town of High Hants itself. There were also the three bubbles attached to the central bubble of the town: the Science Block which regulated the air, the climate, the sun and the seasons; the great prison known as the Marshalsea; and the Ecosphere, where the crops were grown, the cows and chickens and pigs reared. The Ecosphere was reputed to be as large as High Hants itself, if not larger. It was the obvious choice.

49

"Yes, of course," he said.

"The border might be a wee bit tricky, but no one looks properly at a workman. Once you're in, you'll be fine. People don't care what the Ecos do, as long as they get their egg and beans of a morning."

"Yes," Mr Thark said again thoughtfully. "It might work."

"It had better," said Mr Threadneedle. "It's the only plan I've got."

Before Mr Thark could respond, Mr Threadneedle slipped out of the van with a reassuring smile, and he and Frank slammed their doors and Mr Thark and Jenny were alone in the dark.

For a time, there was only silence.

At length, Jenny said, "It'll be all right. Dad knows what he's doing."

"Does he?"

"Yes."

Another silence.

"Mr Thark?"

"Yes?"

"I, I'm sorry about all this. It's my fault. I should never have gone to see Miss Jones."

"Don't worry about that. It's not your fault really. You didn't know what was going to happen. How could you? I'm just sorry I got angry. I didn't mean it."

"Are you sure?"

"Yes. Listen. Collecting all those books all those years? They were bound to find out sooner or later. I always knew it. It's the risk I took."

"All the same. I'm sorry."

"Ah, don't say another word. It's done."

A longer silence followed.

"Mr Thark?"

"Mm?"

"I don't understand what has just happened. I don't understand any of it. And yet I don't think I am stupid."

"No, you're certainly not that. What do you want to know?"

"Well, for one thing... Why are they so desperate to get us? We're not murderers or bank robbers. Speaking to someone you're not supposed to, reading something you shouldn't... these are bad things, I know that. But they're not the worst, are they?"

"Aren't they?"

"Mr Thark, please."

He sighed. "High Hants... this place where we live. You're too close to see what it really is, perhaps. Even I only saw it when it was too late. They hate us, more than murderers and thieves, because of a thought that your Miss Jones has implanted in you."

"What's that?"

"Change, young lady, change. It's the one thing they can't allow."

"You're not making sense."

"Listen. This is how it is. It all started a very long time ago. Long before you were born. No wonder you don't understand. You're like someone trying to make sense of a novel when you've only read the last fifty pages."

"I was taught history at school."

"Not this history."

He took a moment to collect his thoughts, and proceeded.

"Life wasn't always like this. Down on Earth, I mean. It really was all very different. In those times you could say and do anything you wan— No, that's not true. But, for instance, you could say what you liked about the King. Not everyone might love you for it, but they couldn't get you arrested. And you could be whatever you liked, too. Black or white, gay or straight or whatever you like, feminist, chauvinist, fascist, communist, anarchist, Lib Dem or Green. But here, here, you can only be what they want you to be. And I can tell you that coming to this place is the bitterest punishment I could ever have devised for myself."

Jenny digested all this for a space.

"They?" she asked finally. "Who's they?"

"We're sitting underneath their house. This is where they live."

"The Royal Family?"

In the darkness, Jenny could not quite see Mr Thark, but she could just make out his bulk moving and she heard a low snuffling sound. At length he spoke and she realised he was laughing. "They're not Royal, Jenny, any more than you or I," he said with a grim chuckle. "They just happened to be rich and powerful and a little bit cracked, at just the right time.

"I hope you're listening carefully, because I've never said it before and I never will again. It goes against everything I have ever written, everything I have cheered on from the sidelines. I have seen my dreams become monsters and turn against me, as happens in dreams.

"But let me say it, just this once, for the sake of my dead self-respect.

"These men, these fat white men, owned newspapers, TV stations, tech giants. They were bankers and moguls, and some made their money in ways too shady to name. But they lived in a free society where you could say anything and be anything, and they hated that, yes they did, even though it's what made their fortunes. They hated that there was anyone who spoke of them with anything except reverence and awe. And they knew the game was almost up. They had taken so much out of the world that there simply wasn't enough left any more. So they banded together and formed a new company so that, when the time came, they could escape. They would be Princes and their leader would be King, because that's the kind of game spoilt children like, and that's what they were, spoilt children. And they called all this the Lunar Project.

"They dreamed of a colony on another world, made in their own pale image, and it became this place we live in now, High Hants, on the edge of the Sea of Rains. It was required to be absolutely stratified and stable. It would allow of no change at all. After all, we're just one tiny bubble of air on the Moon. We have no resources except what is here already. Change is impossible. Anything that threatens this society of ours in any way, even a single word in the wrong place, has to be punished with the utmost severity. As long as you are absolutely passive and docile, you're safe. But step out of line as we have done, and you're dead meat.

Because, ultimately, the only reason we are here at all is to serve them, the so-called Royals who live in this Palace. Even the poor old King, God rest him."

"Poor old?" asked Jenny, noticing his tone. "The King?"

"The point is, I've got the wrong books on my shelf. You've seen the wrong people. And, well, your father did the best for you, tried to bring you up good and docile, but I'm sorry to say it but it hasn't quite worked, has it?"

"What do you mean?"

"Oh, you know what I mean. You haven't been very docile today."

"I only did what seemed right."

"Yes, exactly. They notice these things."

"Oh."

Their thoughtful silence was broken when the back door was thrown open. They turned in shock; but it was only Mr Threadneedle.

"Change of plan," he said. "You've got to come with us. But not like that. Put some shoes on first. There's some under your seats."

They felt underneath and found two pairs of battered work shoes, heavily weighted for added stability. They put them on. The shoes were big and uncomfortable, but they would suffice. They climbed slowly out of the van and stretched themselves; Mr Thark gave a quiet groan.

Mr Threadneedle looked them over critically. He turned to Mr Thark first. "Take off your jacket, that won't do at all."

"What?"

"The jacket, man. If anyone asks, you're a workman. You can't be a workman in a tweed jacket."

Mr Thark started to stammer a protest. Then he stopped, sighed, and took off the jacket. He plucked a small grey-bound book out of the jacket's inner pocket and slipped into the back pocket of his trousers. He threw the jacket into the back of the van.

Mr Threadneedle nodded and turned to his daughter. She was simply dressed in her teacher's clothes, a white blouse and dark skirt and a

53

cardigan. "Turn your sleeves back," he advised. "You can pass as a lady assistant if needs be." She followed his instructions without protest.

He slammed the van door shut and locked up. "Come on," he said.

As they made their way to the workman's entrance at the far end of the parking area, he said to them in a low tone: "There's an alert on. Security's going round. They'll be checking the van. But don't worry. They won't be looking for us, workmen are furniture. And we can always hide you in a works hatch if we have to."

They went through the door and down a shabby and bare corridor to the lift. Mr Threadneedle selected the button for Floor Six. "Going up," he said cheerfully. "Household goods, soft furnishings, royal apartments." And then, with a ping, the doors opened and they were there.

The walls and the ceilings were painted a rich and soothing lilac; there were ornate cornices; the floor was richly carpeted. The three padded down the passageway silently.

Mr Threadneedle said: "We're down at the end. The lights are on the blink, and no wonder either. The wiring is, well, let's say it wasn't me did the original job. It needs fixing. We can't be taking any chances, can we, not with things as they are."

"No, indeed," said Mr Thark.

Jenny noticed the look which passed between the two men, and said sharply: "What?"

"What is it?" her father asked.

"What are you not telling me? You and Mr Thark keep dropping these hints but you won't *say* it."

Mr Threadneedle stopped walking. "What do you think, Desmond? Should I show her?"

"Show me what?"

"Yes," said Mr Thark, "show her what?" He stopped and a realisation came to him. "You can't mean he's here? On this floor?"

"Of course he is. First on the left."

"Who?" asked Jenny. "A clear and simple explanation will suffice."

54

"Clear and simple, eh?" said Mr Threadneedle. "That could be tricky."

"Have you ever wondered," Mr Thark said, "why we never see the King in public?"

"No," said Jenny. "He's the King."

"But you see the Princes all over the place. Why not the King? I'll tell you why not. It's because he's, he's not well."

"Not fit to be seen," Mr Threadneedle added.

"No. Not for a long time. We're not supposed to know, and no one talks about it. But if you were around when it happened, you know. People talked."

"When?" said Jenny. "What time is this?"

"A long time ago. Twenty years. When we came here to begin with. You see the whole trouble is he would never listen."

"Silly fool," said Mr Threadneedle.

"Yes. Silly fool. He always had to be right, you see. And laughing at health and safety regulations, that was just what he did, wasn't it? So when he blasted off, well, the thing is, he didn't strap himself in properly."

"Broke his neck. Smashed him up. Daft old sod."

"They say he... never regained consciousness. He's just hooked up to life support machines and drips and all that sort of thing."

"So obviously we can't be having anything like a power outage in his vicinity, can we? Tell you what," Mr Threadneedle added. "D'you want to see him? He's just down here. I've looked in on him many a time. He won't bite." He made to walk to the door, but Mr Thark stopped him.

Mr Threadneedle looked at him inquiringly, and Mr Thark nodded over at Jenny.

She was standing there immobile, distressed. A change came over her father's face.

"Oh," he said. "I'm sorry, love. You always did like him, didn't you?"

Jenny found at once her breath coming in short gasps and the light in that plain corridor strangely livid. It was as if the world were crashing about her. Nothing was stable. She could deal with everything Mr Thark had told her, except this. The King was wise; the King was good; the King looked over the people of High Hants from every wall. And the King was on life support, vegetative, his neck broken.

"He's just a picture in a frame," she heard her father say, not unkindly. "You never knew him."

"Get away," said Jenny. "Leave me alone."

The two men stood back, not knowing what to do. Jenny turned her face to the wall and stood there for a minute.

At last, she turned back, and her face was the aftermath of a storm.

"Where are we off to, dad?" she asked.

"Frank's just down here, end of the corridor," said Mr Threadneedle. "We're quite safe, no one comes on this floor except—"

His voice trailed off as he stared down the passageway. Jenny brought her head up to look. She saw a tall, suited figure. First it stood at the end of the passage, and then it started walking towards them, not hurrying but with purpose.

Mr Threadneedle turned and said, "Come on, let's go this way..." He was about to lead them back the way they had come, but they saw at the same time another figure at the other end, suited like the first, but with a clipped brown moustache, also walking towards them slowly and purposefully.

"Miss Threadneedle," Goffin called out. "How lovely to see you again."

"This way!" said Mr Threadneedle, and the next moment, before Jenny realised it, they were inside the King's Apartment.

"No!" she exclaimed, turning back, but it was already too late. She heard a loud bang on the door just as her father tried to close it, and in the next moment Goffin's companion threw the door open and entered. He had a gun in his hand.

"Don't move," he advised.

Jenny was aware of a low electric hum and a rhythmic hiss of air, but she refused to look at the bed which she knew was against the far wall.

She was staring first at the man, and then at Goffin who was suddenly there too, a satisfied grin on his face.

"Now then," he said. "What have we here? It's looks like an act of lèse-majesté to me. What do you say, Barnsley?"

"Bang to rights, sah," said the man called Barnsley.

"Yes, bang, as you say, to rights. So," Goffin continued, approaching the three and giving them an openly contemptuous look, "and is this the best they can do? Really? A nursery nurse and two raddled old men? Is this really the pink and flower of the resistance of which we hear so much?"

"No," said Mr Thark.

"Quiet!" Goffin shouted with crazy suddenness in Mr Thark's face. "I will not be spoken to! Especially not by some drink-sodden old soak, some pathetic castrated-liberal hack, some, some, some..."

"Fourth-rate lickspittle snowflake? Sausage-fingered lamebrain?" Mr Thark suggested.

"Quiet!"

"Only trying to help."

"Shut up! Barnsley!"

"Sah!"

"Take these three, these, these, and just... take them away, won't you?"

"Where, sir?"

There was a movement in the background, but Jenny found herself transfixed by Goffin. He seemed to deflate before her eyes as his madness faded. "Oh, anywhere," he said sadly, "anywhere, as long as it's out of my sight. Just looking at them makes me want to vomit."

And it was at this moment, as Barnsley's gun came up once more, that Jenny properly noticed the thin, elegant man who had appeared in the doorway, as he walked leisurely into the room and drawled in a quiet, authoritative voice: "Now what is going on here?"

CHAPTER TEN: Unravelling

THE OTHER FOUR SNAPPED THEIR heads round. Goffin was for a moment speechless.

"Far be it for me to seem to be inquisitive," the man went on, "but one cannot help but wonder what exactly you are all doing in the King's Apartment."

There was a strained pause.

He walked forward with complete assurance. He was very tall and slender, exquisitely tailored, with a mild and slightly unworldly face topped with a shock of dark hair slicked well back. He was perhaps twenty years older than he pretended. He walked with a slim black stick.

"Well?" he said.

Barnsley had lowered the gun as soon as he saw the newcomer and was trying to look invisible. Goffin, however, was made of sterner stuff, and marched up to him and snarled: "What's it to you?"

"I wonder," said the man, "if you know who you are talking to."

"No," said Goffin, "and I don't –"

"It's Prince Osric," Mr Thark murmured behind him. "You call him 'your royal highness'."

"Ah," said Goffin. He stood for a second; then a weak smile crawled across his face. "Your royal highness. You see, it's like this..."

"I would suggest," said the Prince, "before we go any further with what I am sure is a fascinating explanation, that we retire from the royal presence."

"I'm sorry?"

58

"The King," said the Prince mildly. "I really do hope you are aware that you are standing barely ten feet away from the King."

Now there was definitely panic in Goffin's eyes. "Oh yes, yes, of course, you're quite right, we should retire, yes, let's go into the corridor. Barnsley." He gestured to his henchman, who began to usher the others out of the room, as Goffin stood back to allow them to go first. But all at once the Prince strode forward and, viciously slashing Barnsley's legs with his stick, yelled: "Backwards, you little shit! You retire from the King's presence backwards!"

"Sodding hell," said Barnsley, buckling at the knees.

What followed was an embarrassed regrouping. Jenny, instructed to face the King and to leave the royal presence in reverse, bowing as she went, was forced for the first time to see the thing she had been avoiding. It was not, in the end, as bad as she had imagined. The high bed and its white blankets, the machines, the drips and the wires almost obscured altogether the sad, shrunken figure in the middle, its skin so pale that it was almost grey, its eyes closed, its small chest rising and falling. In a moment she was outside in the corridor with the others and the King could no longer be seen.

The tale that Goffin was spinning for the Prince was a strange rigmarole indeed, of dissidence and revolt, subversive elements in our very schools, forbidden texts, of a lone voice of truth and decency pitched against a veritable avalanche of filth. Most of it came as complete news to her.

"I see, I see," said the Prince, closing his eyes. "What a very fine fellow you must be, to be sure. And these are your dangerous subversives here are they? Well, well." He sauntered down the line, first Mr Threadneedle, then Jenny, and finally—

"Oh, hello, Thark. You here?"

"Yes, your royal highness."

"Jolly good." He started to move away, then looked back. "I didn't think you were a radical, Thark."

"Oh, no, sir, I'm not."

"This *gentleman* seems to think you are."

"Yes, sir."

"Very odd."

"Yes, sir."

"You're sure you're not a radical, Thark?"

"Quite sure, sir. Indeed, if anything, the opposite."

"But this fellow here, what's his name? Goffin? This Goffin seems convinced that you and your friends are some sort of terrorist cell."

"Yes, sir."

"Well, what d'you make of that?"

"Well, it's not for me to say, sir, of course, but I wonder if it might be a matter of mistaken identity. You know me, sir, a very harmless chap. This is Miss Jenny Threadneedle, sir, she teaches English at primary level, and this is her father, Jack, a most capable fellow, an electrician. Jenny lives in the same lodging-house as me. We talk about books sometimes."

"Books? What books?"

"Jane Austen, sir."

The Prince threw up his hands and barked with laughter. "Oh, this is nonsense! You, Goffin, you're an ass. You're to let these fellows go now, you understand?"

"But..." said Goffin, bewildered.

"Do you understand?" the Prince repeated.

"Yes, your royal highness," said Goffin miserably.

"Jolly good," said the Prince, smiling. "Jane Austen! I ask you! Well, ta-ta, Thark, ta-ta..." He started down the corridor, all smiles, and Jenny found herself smiling stupidly in response just as her father and Mr Thark started giggling helplessly in the face of Goffin's discomfiture; and the Prince stopped in his tracks, and, turning, said in a puzzled tone, "Thark?"

"Sir?"

"You write for the *Gazette*, don't you? You write as Tom Tattle."

Mr Thark's smile was perhaps a trifle fixed as he replied, "Yes, sir."

"I thought so." The Prince wandered back, and the dreamy look was in his eyes again, that look which Jenny was beginning to recognise as a danger signal. He was standing directly in front of Mr Thark now, and he murmured mildly: "'Endured'?"

"Sir?"

"'Having endured a most interesting talk.' I think that was the phrase, wasn't it?"

"A typo, sir. That should be 'enjoyed', of course. I was very angry when I saw what they'd printed."

"I see, I see. A typo, eh?"

"Yes, sir. There'll be a correction this week. I'll insist on it."

"Oh, I would, Thark, I would. A very unfortunate word to misspell, and when you think of it, quite hard to do." He stood in thought for a moment; and then, without any change of expression, slapped Mr Thark hard across the face.

Turning away, he addressed Goffin. "Take them away," he said.

"Yes, your royal highness, with pleasure," Goffin said happily. "Well, you bastards, you heard his royal highness. Come on."

The prisoners were silent in the police van as it trundled and bumped towards their fate at the great prison of Marshalsea. Mr Thark seemed oddly deflated, and even Jenny's father, whom she had never known to be discouraged, had a gloomy look about him. As for Jenny herself, she was simply stunned and bewildered by the reversals of the past few hours. The foundations had shifted. She had difficulty making sense of the day's mad chase. Why had she even started running? It had come to the same thing in the end. It was all as in a novel where explanations had to be made in the last chapter. Only then could the unravelling occur and the happy endings be handed out. She sat back on the bench and closed her eyes against the hard world, awaiting the plot's final resolution.

CHAPTER ELEVEN: Nor Iron Bars a Cage

UPON ARRIVAL AT THE MARSHALSEA, they were searched for offensive weapons. They were deprived of their clothes and told to don the prison uniform instead. However, they were permitted to retain their personal possessions.

Jenny was led to a spartan but functional cell with a bed, wash stand, and toilet. The door was slammed upon her and the lock was turned.

She sat on the bed and looked for almost ten minutes at the opposite wall, painted a yellow colour that reminded her of childhood illness. She lay down on the bed for a further five minutes. She stood up and wandered over to the door, which had a small grille set in it at face height, covered at the moment with a closed hatch operable from the other side. Having checked that the door was indeed locked, she returned to the bed and sat down once more.

She took from her pocket the card bearing the photographs of her mother, and she looked at them unblinkingly and almost blankly for some time.

The face that looked back at her seemed to her more defiant in its attitude than she had noticed. Who, after all, was this woman who was half of her? Why had she refused to join her husband and her daughter in their journey to new life on the Moon? What could the Earth have been to her that she could not bear to leave it? Could she have somehow known what the Moon had in store for them?

The door was unlocked and opened. The guard gestured to Jenny to follow her, and Jenny followed her. She was led to an interrogation room and guided inside. The door was shut behind her.

Goffin was seated at the table.

"Do sit down," he said.

Jenny sat down in the chair facing Goffin.

"I haven't done anything wrong," she said.

Goffin smiled pleasantly. "Oh, we've gone far beyond that, Miss Threadneedle. That isn't even on the table."

"So what do you want of me?"

"What do I want. Well, you can sit there and listen to me. I'm going to tell you exactly what is going to happen to you. You will go back to your cell and you will face trial. You will not be asked to attend the hearing, because nothing you can say will make the slightest difference. You will be found guilty, naturally. Some days after this, you will be taken and sedated and you will be thrown out of the airlock onto the surface of the Moon. Perhaps you don't know what happens to a body when it goes out of an airlock. It is very interesting. The air in your lungs expands catastrophically, causing the lungs to rupture. The lack of atmospheric pressure results in your blood literally boiling. It is curious to reflect on that. I am not even mentioning the effect that lack of oxygen has upon your ability to breathe; one takes that as read. Needless to say, you die within a few seconds. I like to think that the person wakes before death just in time to experience something of those last moments. That would be somehow satisfying, don't you think. I think that's all."

Goffin went to the door and opened it. He said to the guard: "Take her back."

So Jenny was returned to her cell.

The following days were uneventful. Jenny was woken at seven o'clock, following which a meal was provided through a slot in the door, consisting usually of spam, egg and beans with a glass of water – a great improvement on breakfast at Mrs Cardigan's. Every second day, her uniform was swapped with a clean replacement. A quiet morning with a book from the King's Library was interrupted only by lunch, a slice of toast and marge served with milky tea. The library trolley passed at about four-thirty, affording Jenny the opportunity to exchange her book. At six, soup with a crust of dry bread and another glass of water. Lights out at eight-thirty. Jenny was usually asleep by nine.

She did not think of the future, knowing there was none. She took some comfort in the books she reread. The cadence of the sentences, as familiar as a well-loved landscape, soothed her through their very familiarity. She was not happy, of course. The sheer unreason of her circumstances left her beached and gasping. But she had lived most of her life in acceptance of things, and she could see no other response to what was happening now.

On the sixth day, the door was opened. "Come with me," said the guard.

She was led down many strange corridors. They seemed to be walking a long while; at least ten minutes. At length, they came to the dead end of a passage. The end wall bore a great steel door with many rivets, painted a vivid green. The guard beat on the door. After a few seconds, Jenny heard a deep clanking sound, the rattling of many keys, and a further deep clank. The door slowly and heavily swung inwards. The guard on the other side gestured to them to come through.

They were now standing in another long passage. The walls and ceiling were painted cream, and the tiles on the floor were white. At the far end of the passage there was another steel door, just like the one they had just passed through except that it was painted red.

The guards guided her to a door which was set into the right-hand wall about halfway along the passage. One of the guards opened the door and ushered her through into a large, empty room. This guard then left.

She was alone. There was no table or chair, not even a window or a grille. All there was was the door through which she had come.

Five minutes later, the door opened again. A new figure was led in and abandoned. "Dad!" Jenny exclaimed, and embraced him, much to his embarrassment.

"I reckon this is it," he said.

"I'm sorry, dad," Jenny said. "This is all my fault."

"Don't be daft. You never did anything wrong."

"You shouldn't have come after me."

"But I'm your dad."

Next in was Mr Thark. He was very much the worse for wear after a week in prison – unshaven, shabby, and unwashed.

"Oh, hello," he said vaguely. "Together again for the big finish, eh?"

They stared at the door, awaiting the next event, increasingly puzzled. Why had they been brought here and left? This was not how they had imagined their end. Surely, if they were to be led away and executed, it should be done one at a time; not like this, where they were left free and unbound, and they would have the advantage over any guard now entering. What was the point?

Their thoughts, such as they were, were interrupted once more by the opening of the door and the arrival of another newcomer, quite as grubby and tired-looking as the others. Thark stared at her blankly. "Who are you? What is this?" Mr Threadneedle was scarcely less bewildered.

Jenny stepped forward. "Miss Jones!" she exclaimed. "I thought you were dead!"

"A fine way to greet an old friend!" said Miss Jones, but with a smile, as she opened her arms and embraced Jenny.

"It's all rather mysterious," Miss Jones continued. "I thought these people were models of efficiency. But it's been almost a fortnight. Maybe they want to prolong the agony. It would be just like them."

Jenny looked round the room. They were certainly a motley crew: her father, short and solid and dependable; Mr Thark, large, flabby and slightly collapsed; and Miss Jones, tall and slim and ramrod-straight, even in this extremity. And what had brought them together in the face of death? Nothing but a few incautious words. They had harmed no one, stolen nothing. Their only crime was... was what? The smallest possible itch of discontent. It was all a farce; and Jenny had never found farce to be especially funny.

The door opened once more. Four guards entered the room silently. They were armed. They stood at the corners of the room and waited. After a pause, a fifth guard entered and addressed the prisoners.

"Follow me," she said.

A moment's hesitation, and Miss Jones moved first to the leave the room. The others went after her. They were led to the right, down the corridor and towards the red door. The four armed guards were behind them. They had nowhere to flee to.

They stood before the red door. As before, the leading guard rapped on its metal. Again the prisoners heard that clank and rattle. The red door swung open. With terror in their hearts, and seeing no escape, the prisoners stepped through.

CHAPTER TWELVE: The Other Side

WHAT CONFRONTED THEM ON THE other side of the door took their breath away.

Jenny was not quite sure what she had expected. Perhaps some dark chamber, an ante-room to the airlock that would be their last place of rest; perhaps a bright and lurid operating room where they would be sedated by some cackling doctor in a gown and mask; perhaps a place of torture, heavy with chains and racks.

What she saw instead was this: a great space, larger than she could quite compute, spotlessly clean and shining with the dazzling white of its surfaces: a vast dome, its girdered arches and struts undisguised and unhidden, and swarming with white-clad people.

They were standing on something like a raised platform. A rail protected them from the drop into the arena below. The platform stretched to either side and gave access to arches set in the side of the dome. This platform appeared to extend all the way round the dome.

The guard who had led them through turned to them and said, "Stay here. You will be taken care of." She marched away and through one of the near arches.

"Now what?" said Mr Thark. "The suspense is becoming tedious."

They became slowly more aware of the details of their surroundings. They heard the echoing susurration of hundreds of workers going about their work, accompanied by the faint whisper of machinery at a great distance, and, deeper than this, a low, slow thud or groan, its origin not discoverable, its meaning scarcely even guessable. The four of them huddled closer as their nameless fear grew.

A figure emerged from an archway and approached. She was a woman of about sixty years of age, lean and fit, with short silver hair and dressed, like everyone else, entirely in white.

"Good morning," she said. "Please do not be afraid. You are quite safe. Step this way."

The group followed her through the arch and into her office. Their arrival had clearly been expected: four chairs had been arranged before the desk. She gestured for them to sit. As they did so, she seated herself on the other side.

"My name," she said, "is Popkiss. Ursula Popkiss, but you can call me Doctor. First of all, let me give you a definitive assurance that you are *not* going to be executed. Unless, of course, you especially wish it, in which case please do let me know and I will be more than happy to arrange matters to your satisfaction.

"You will want to know where you are. There is no name for this place, because officially it does not exist. However, I can tell you that we, that is, we and our predecessors, designed and engineered the space programme which facilitated the building and populating of High Hants. Once that was accomplished, we were expunged from the record. Our purpose, as far as the Royal Family was concerned, was complete. Nevertheless, we found it inconvenient to destroy ourselves, and, as you can see, here we are. This our humble abode is situated on the far side of the Marshalsea, some distance apart from High Hants, and attached to it only through the prison itself.

"In any event, and despite the absence of official sanction, our usefulness was not entirely over. We are, after all, scientists. Observations and data are our meat and drink. Our new circumstances are of great use to the inquiring mind."

She paused, smiling again, and took a sip from a glass of water.

"This is all very interesting," said Mr Thark, "but..."

Dr Popkiss held up a hand. "Please. I am going to tell you everything, but I must tell you in my own way.

"As you know, High Hants was created to be stable and changeless. However, in the event, things were not so simple. When are they ever? People change, even when they think they do not. It has been interesting to see the process by which the reactionary becomes the radical."

"I don't know why you are looking at me," said Mr Thark.

"Don't you? Well, in any case, it is a fact that discontent has been brewing in High Hants, and it is now almost at the boil."

"I haven't heard anything about that," said Jenny. "Everything seems to be quite as normal."

"Of course," said Dr Popkiss. "No one reports it, obviously. That is what suppression means."

"It wouldn't matter if everyone knew anyway," said Mr Thark bitterly. "It's not as if there's any alternative."

"No?"

"Of course there isn't. Where would we go?"

Dr Popkiss shrugged. "Why, Earth, of course."

There was a sudden hush. Dr Popkiss was leaning back in her chair, and the four others were staring at her in frank astonishment. Mr Thark was ready with a tart response, but it died on his lips as a thought occurred to him which struck him silent.

He examined this thought of his and turned it over and looked at it from every side. Finally, he said quietly: "I see."

Then, after a further pause, he continued, picking his way: "That's why we're here, of course. You want us to go to Earth. That's why we've been plucked from Death Row and delivered to you. It's all very convenient. What have we got to lose?"

"What indeed," said Miss Jones. "Only, you see, I remember when we left Earth, and I'm sure you do too. That planet was dying. I don't want to be thrown onto a dead planet."

"No," said Dr Popkiss. She considered for a moment, then she stood up. "Follow me."

She led them out of her office and down the passage to a door which was labelled: "Annexe 3." She stepped through, and the others followed.

They were in an almost circular room, ringed with desks of controls. Before them, the walls were glazed with large windows which looked straight out onto the bleak landscape of the Moon. Above them was a clear dome interrupted by a great instrument which seemed to pierce the dome's skin. The instrument had an eyepiece below at the correct level. There was a team of workers in white who moved to and fro between the eyepiece and the controls and a coffee-maker in an alcove.

"Here," said Dr Popkiss, "we observe. The Moon, the Earth, the stars and the planets. Look. You don't even need the telescope to see this."

She led them to the far window and they gaped at the sight. It was a view such as they had never seen, a craggy landscape of grey and silver and black. And there, hanging in the sky, high and huge, was a misty, cloudy globe, many-coloured and impossibly detailed, white and blue and green and all else. At the sight of it, every heart skipped.

"There it is," said Dr Popkiss. "Home."

They stood in silence for a long time. The technicians bustled around them; one of them gently encouraged Miss Jones to shift slightly to the right so she could take a reading.

At length, Mr Thark said: "That's all very well."

"Yes, it is, isn't it?"

"But, with respect, it doesn't alter the main point."

Dr Popkiss turned to him with controlled exasperation. "Mr Thark. Do you think these instruments are here for show?"

"I wouldn't put it past you."

She made a visible decision to stay calm. "We have been observing and monitoring conditions on Earth for a considerable time. Our observations show that it remains habitable in the temperate zones. We have seen signs that human life is in fact thriving on the surface."

The technician looked up, startled. "I don't think that's..."

Dr Popkiss stopped her with a glance. "It is not inconsistent with our readings."

The technician looked at her, and decided not to make any further remarks on the subject. She moved off quickly.

Dr Popkiss went on: "Of course, the only way to be absolutely sure is to go there. We will take every precaution for your safe arrival."

She provided further details of the plan. They were to launch from the Moon to the Lunar Project's space station which circled the Moon eternally, officially named Pilgrim but known to all as Watford Gap. The vessel would then execute a directed launch from Watford Gap into the Earth's atmosphere for splashdown in the North Sea.

"But you can't possibly ask us to control a spaceship," Mr Thark said.

"Of course not," Dr Popkiss replied. "We would scarcely trust you with such a sophisticated piece of technology. One of our most respected team members will accompany you. Once on Earth we would merely ask you to report any findings back to us. We will provide you with a transmitter."

"The North Sea?" Mr Thark asked, without a response.

They were back in Dr Popkiss's office now, and she leaned back in her chair and said, "Well, what do you say? Will you go?"

"I don't know why you're asking," Mr Thark said at last. "It's not as if we have a choice."

"There is always a choice," said Dr Popkiss.

"Oh, yes. Silly me."

Miss Jones said: "This is ridiculous. Of course I'll do it. It's what I've dreamed of, for ever so long. I only want to return to Earth."

"Good," said Dr Popkiss. She turned to the others. "And you?"

After a pause, Mr Threadneedle spoke up. "You don't need me. I'm more use here than I'd ever be on Earth. There's a lot of wiring still needs fixing."

"But, Mr Threadneedle. That is not an option. You will be executed."

"Why? I've done nothing wrong."

"Really?" Dr Popkiss picked up a file and looked through it. "I understand that you have seen the King."

71

"Why, yes. What's that got to do with..." His voice trailed off. "I see," he said quietly.

Mr Thark intervened. "May I suggest something?" he said. "Does Jack have to return to High Hants? Couldn't he be of use to you yourselves? Don't you need electricians here, in this ridiculous science dome of yours?"

Dr Popkiss considered. "It's possible," she said. "I shall have to consult with my colleagues."

"Do."

Then Mr Thark said: "As for myself... if I must die, it might as well be this way. Count me in."

"Good enough," said Dr Popkiss. "Welcome to the team."

Jenny was sitting with her eyes downcast, but she could feel Dr Popkiss's eyes on her. It seemed her head was nothing more than a confused jumble. As she sat there undecided, there came to her all at once an image, the portrait of her mother in that far-off photo booth, and in her mind she reached out to it like a lifeline.

"Yes," Jenny murmured. "Yes, I'll go."

CHAPTER THIRTEEN: Going Home

THEY WERE SHOWN THEIR QUARTERS, small rooms scarcely larger than their cells but clean and airy, and without locks on the doors. They were reunited with the clothes they had worn when they had been arrested. Even Mr Thark's tweed jacket was returned to him; he could not imagine how.

They were introduced to their new companion who would be navigating them back to Earth. She was Dr Parveen Akhtar, a small, dark-skinned young woman who bore patiently with the momentary bewilderment on Jenny's face and Mr Thark's visible efforts to bite back the offensive remark that sprang to his lips.

"My mother's family came from Pakistan originally," she explained to Miss Jones. "She was part of the original Lunar team. Almost my earliest memories are of this place. They have been very considerate. After all, my mother's expertise was invaluable to them. She died last year."

"I'm sorry."

"Of course, I could never be permitted to live in High Hants itself. But I have been very happy here in the Science Quarter. Indeed I have. I have been educated to be part of the team. I will be sad to leave them."

"But all the same, you asked to leave?"

"Oh yes."

Over the next few days, Miss Jones, Mr Thark and Jenny were given intensive training in advance of their journey: mostly to ensure they remained properly strapped and did not attempt any unnecessary movement. The training went well.

On the second day of their new life, Mr Thark was in his room, resting his eyes on the pages of his book, when Jenny visited him.

"I'm sorry to disturb you," she said.

"You're not disturbing me," he replied, marking his page with a ribbon. He set the book down on the table.

"What's that?" Jenny asked.

Mr Thark touched the little grey volume briefly and smiled. "The last of my library."

Jenny read the spine. "*Alice's Adventures in Wonderland and Through the Looking Glass.* May I look?"

"Be my guest."

She picked it up and looked through the pages. "Pictures?"

"Of course. What's the use of a book without pictures and conversations?"

"It looks like a children's book."

"It is."

Jenny was stricken again with remorse. "I'm so sorry, Mr Thark."

"No, no. It's the only book I really ever needed. It tells me all I will ever know about the world."

She turned to a random page, and read: "'He's in prison now, being punished: and the trial doesn't even begin till next Wednesday: and of course the crime comes last of all.'"

Mr Thark grinned and spread his arms. "You see?" he said.

Next day, they were shown the vessel that would be bearing them on their journey. The greater part of its bulk consisted of the engine, which was topped with a surprisingly small pod, just large enough to contain them. "The rockets will be mostly used to take us up to the space station," Dr Akhtar explained. "Of course the Moon's weak gravity is on our side there. The rockets will also boost us on our re-entry into the Earth's atmosphere."

Jenny did not even attempt to understand most of the explanations that were given. Her role was to sit still and accept events, a role for which she was well trained.

"You were made to be an angel in the house," said Miss Jones.

Jenny replied, "Thank you," and Miss Jones looked at her oddly.

Once, after lunch at the canteen, Jenny found that she and Miss Jones were alone at the table. She realised they had not really talked since that fateful time at the Lyons tea house.

The same thought seemed to have occurred to Miss Jones, and she smiled at Jenny ruefully. "I suppose you could say this is all my fault. I can only tell you I meant it all for the best. What a hollow sound those words make. I'm sorry."

"There's nothing to be sorry for," said Jenny, realising as she said it that it was true. "What else was I going to do with my life? I should be thanking you. After all, I'm going home."

Jenny was drinking the last of her tea. Miss Jones lifted her own teacup and clinked it against Jenny's. "Home," she said. "May it be all we need it to be."

Jenny looked at her thoughtfully for a while, and said: "I don't understand you."

"What don't you understand? I'm absurdly simple really."

"Why did you do it? You seemed so... dependable. And then suddenly you threw it all away. You hadn't even finished your Bakewell tart."

Miss Jones's mouth twitched in a silent laugh. "Maybe that was the last straw. But the truth is, the idea had been in my mind for days, weeks. I didn't know I was going to do it just then. Perhaps it was you, your, do you mind if I call it naivety? A moment of disgust that overcame me. I tried to warn you, you know."

"I know."

"And I did make sure you were safe. You weren't my accomplice. I made sure you called the police. You were my informant. You should have been quite safe, if only..."

"If only I hadn't visited you. I know. But I had to. I couldn't abandon you, I liked you. I still do."

"Good."

"And when they arrested you... did you think you were going to die?"

"Yes, of course. What else?"

Jenny looked at her, wondering, and at last she asked softly:

"Is it really so bad? Living in High Hants?"

For what seemed a long time, Miss Jones sat without speaking. Then she appeared to make a decision in her mind, and she nodded and said:

"Yes. I don't think, even now, you realise what High Hants really is. But then, how could you? You don't remember Earth."

"I don't understand," said Jenny. "What do you mean?"

Miss Jones sighed. "Everyone in High Hants is white, Jenny."

"Well, yes, I know that. I've lived there all my life, almost."

"Yes, exactly. You know it, but you don't *see* it. The men who made High Hants only wanted one kind of citizen, their own kind. They let us in not because we were so sweet and virtuous and lovable but because they liked the colour of our skins. That's the truth of it. They wanted everyone else to *die*. The black and the brown, the yellow and the olive. And, Jenny, we just went along with it. We thanked our lucky stars that our skin was the right colour and we blanked out the rest. It's surprising what a person can stomach when she has to, isn't it? Except, you see, there does come a time, sometimes, when the stomach rebels. One day, not long ago, I realised I'd had enough of the whole thing. That's all."

Miss Jones set down her teacup and smiled.

"Come on," she said, standing. "The others will be wanting to know where we are."

Jenny frequently visited the Maintenance Quarter, where her father was stationed. He was usually to be found in the common room playing a game of cards with his colleagues. There was a sort of jocular intensity to their style of play which Jenny found oddly reassuring. They were all men, and they were all in some strange way exactly like him; it was nothing she could quite put her finger on, for they were different ages, and different sizes and shapes; perhaps it was a look in their eye, or perhaps it was something else.

She knew these would be the last days she would ever see him, and she wanted to make the most of them. Maybe he had something of the same feeling, but he seemed almost to avoid being alone with her.

A week had passed, and it was the end of another visit. She had to return to join the others for their group training. (These sessions were mostly variations on yoga and meditation; the most important skill required for the journey, it appeared, would be the ability to keep still.) She stood up, and said "Well, Dad," and he said, "Well, lass," and he escorted her out into the passageway. "Always lovely to see you," he said.

"Yes, Dad," said Jenny. "You, too."

An awkward silence fell.

"Dad," Jenny said. She did not want to speak, but she knew she must. How many more days would there be? How many more chances to talk?

"Aye?" he said.

"Dad," she repeated. "Won't you come with us?"

"Oh no," he said. "I don't think that would do at all. I'm better off here."

"But don't you want to go back to Earth? It's where we're from. Don't you miss it?"

His eyes seemed to drift off for a moment to some other place.

"Well, of course I miss it," he said at last. "But that's different. I can't go back there. All that, the stuff I miss, it's gone forever. Going down to Earth in a tin can won't bring it back. No. I need to stay here. At least I'll be a bit of use this way."

Jenny nodded slowly. "All right," she said. "I understand that. But don't you want to know?"

"Know? Know what?"

Jenny scarcely knew how to put what she wanted to say, but she plunged in anyway. "Well, you know... what happened to the people left behind... I mean people like... well, like mum?"

He was still looking away, down the passage and into nothingness. He was quite still, and yet she saw something change in him. At length, he said:

"No. I don't want to know, I don't want to think about it. You mustn't ask me. I'm not proud of what we did, but we decided it together, Martha and I, we agreed. She couldn't come with us. She had to stay, she said. But we did what was best for you. You've been better off here than you'd ever have been down there. Trust me."

This was new; this was not what he had told her before. But all the same, now that he said it, she realised she had known it, or something like it, for ever. Yes, yes. That was how it must have been, after all.

She looked at him and for a moment he looked at her too. She took his hand.

"Come with me, dad," she said. "Come and let's find mum together."

He shook his head. "No, I'm sorry. I can't."

"But why not?"

"Because," he said, "I know what we'd find."

"What?" she asked, but he just looked into her eyes and shook his head.

That was not the last time they spoke, but Jenny hugged him as if it were.

The day arrived almost too quickly. The dome's arena was cleared; the space vessel was placed in its centre; gantries were erected.

The four voyagers – Jenny, Mr Thark, Miss Jones and Dr Akhtar – made their way to the craft. They took off their heavy boots, then they nimbly scaled the gantry and climbed through the pod's small door into the impossibly cramped space. They strapped themselves in as they had been instructed. The hatch hissed shut and sealed itself. The gantries were withdrawn.

A piercing alarm rang through the dome. All personnel hurried out of the arena. After ten minutes, once all was clear, the doors round the edge of the dome were automatically shut and sealed.

Slowly, with infinite care and grandeur, the dome peeled back to left and right, section upon section, like the lids of an enormous eye, until the unimaginable depths of the pool of space into which they were about to plunge hung naked above them, black and cold and immaculate.

Dr Akhtar, seated at the controls, could just make out through the small viewing panel by her head the faces of the team standing in the launch control room, the window of which looked over the arena. She could see, amongst those faces, those of Dr Popkiss and Jenny's father.

She opened the radio link with Control.

"Ready?"

"Ready."

She flicked switches, and there was a low and rising hum. She started the engines. The whining, roaring sound shuddered through the pod. The whole structure started to vibrate at a deep, deep frequency that became part of them.

"God in heaven," Mr Thark muttered. Jenny shut her eyes and grasped her armrests tighter.

Dr Akhtar changed the radio link. "Watford Gap? Are you reading me, Watford Gap?"

After a long pause, the voice came through, crackly but cheerful. "That's us. Hello, Joyride. Reading you loud and clear."

"Hello, Joe."

"It's Ben, actually."

"Hello, Ben. Ready for us?"

"We've dusted the mantelpiece for you special."

"Good." Dr Akhtar flicked two switches, adjusted the throttle, and placed her hand on the big lever. "We're on our way."

And the engines roared and the flames and dust and burnt fragments blasted the arena and the fragile craft called Joyride lurched horribly and suddenly and with shocking velocity shot up away from High Hants and the Moon and into the void.

CHAPTER FOURTEEN: Pebble in the Sky

BEN AND JOE, WHOSE LIVES were spent staffing the space station called Watford Gap, were men of truly remarkable laziness. Indeed, this was the quality that made them ideal for their job, which was to idle away their entire lives in a sealed container two hundred and thirty-eight thousand miles above the surface of the Earth, accompanied only by an automatic air-recycling plant, enough food and drink to last them a hundred years, electronic devices bearing an inexhaustible supply of pulp fiction, blockbuster movies, and second-rate music, and each other. They were also required to give grudging welcome to any visitors who might be passing on their way to or from the Moon. In this, as all else, they were prepared to do their bit, when there was no other option available.

"Pod closing."

"Left a bit."

"Whoa there."

"Nicely does it. Just a smidge closer."

"There she blows."

"Bullseye!"

The pod attached itself to the space station, their entrance hatches aligning perfectly.

"Come on in and meet the gang!"

The four found they had been holding their breaths without realising it. Now that they were safely docked, they exhaled in a simultaneous gesture of relief.

Dr Akhtar was the first to open the hatch and enter the slim stick of the space station. Ben was there to greet them. "Welcome to our humble abode," he said. "Have a Malteser. They're only a bit manky."

There was not much room, but they were sincerely glad to have an opportunity to stretch for a few minutes and take a comfort break ("Loo's first on the left"). They had a very precise departure slot arranged in an hour's time. Joe was in charge of coordination. Dr Akhtar looked slightly uneasy on learning this.

Half an hour later, Jenny said: "Shouldn't we be strapping ourselves back in?"

"Oh, you've got bags of time," said Joe. "It'll only take you five minutes to get yourselves ready, tops."

"Are you sure?"

"Trust me, we've done this loads of times," said Joe, tinkering with the controls. Ben drew in his breath sharply, and at that moment Jenny noticed the odd thing in what had just been said.

She turned to him and asked, "I'm sorry?"

"Hmm?"

"You've done this loads of times... before?"

Joe smiled at her disarmingly. "Sorry, shouldn't have mentioned it."

"He's joking," said Ben.

"That's it, I'm joking."

Five minutes later, Mr Thark drew Joe to one side. "All right, so how many missions have there been before us?"

Joe looked at Mr Thark. "Four," he said.

"What happened to them?"

"I don't think you should be asking that question."

"You're right. What happened to them?"

Joe shrugged. "Don't know. They never got back to us."

Mr Thark floated away from him, a thoughtful expression on his face. He did not speak to the others for some time.

Ben was at the controls and Miss Jones was with him.

"We don't have to do anything really," he said cheerfully. "We just go round and round the Moon and make sure we don't crash into the others."

"The others? There are other space stations?"

"Oh, for sure. You know. There's the Americans, the Chinese, the Russians..."

"What? I thought it was just us!"

He looked at her, surprised. "Why would you think that?"

She considered this, and said: "I don't know."

"They've all got bases down there. It's funny really. None of them knows about the others. Good job too, I suppose. It prevents, you know, tension."

"Yes, I can see that."

Later, Mr Thark was with Dr Akhtar.

"Dr Akhtar, may I ask you something?"

"Sure."

"When we come down to earth..."

"Yes?"

"We're scheduled to land in the North Sea."

"Yes."

"Big place, the North Sea."

"Yes."

"So, I was just wondering..."

"Yes?"

"How do we get out of it?"

Dr Akhtar looked at him, surprised. "We drift," she said.

Mr Thark did not respond. Frankness was, he knew, a fault of his; and there was no point in being frank at this time, now that there was no going back. However, he found himself considering their chances anew, and he did not like the conclusions he reached.

They returned to the pod, closed the seals, and strapped themselves back in. Dr Akhtar spoke with Joe.

"Zero minus sixty seconds."

"All set."

The countdown began. Jenny breathed slow and deep. She tried to imagine all was well. She could hear Mr Thark, seated next to her, muttering to himself. He seemed to be saying something about slithy toves and mome raths.

"Two, one, zero."

"Contact."

"Cast off."

"Thar she blows!"

"Bon voyage!"

The little craft detached itself from Watford Gap. With the aid of tiny boosts, it manoeuvred itself to a safe distance from the space station.

Dr Akhtar's concentration was total. She flicked the switches and adjusted the settings, all the time checking coordinates and timings. At last, she was ready.

"Okay," she told the others. "Here's what happens now. We have to enter the atmosphere at a shallow angle so that the friction of the atmosphere itself slows us down. This will allow us to splash down safely in the North Sea. We are already in high orbit and this will help us to achieve the correct angle. But we'll still need an extra boost, and that's where the engines come in again. Once that's achieved, we'll eject the engines. It may be," she added, flicking a couple more switches, "a little bit bumpy."

There was a deep judder in the heart of the craft. It jolted forward as if (as it was) rocket-propelled. Jenny's breath was knocked out of her. She wanted to draw breath again but there was no respite, they were accelerating at a terrifying rate and the pressure on her chest increased second by second. With great effort and strain she drew air into her lungs. The shudders and groans increased for seconds that felt like hours. As the conviction stole over her that what she was experiencing was unbearable, there was a great bang and all at once the shuddering and the acceleration stopped, as the engines fell away from the pod.

There was a great sigh of relief through the craft from Jenny, Mr Thark and Miss Jones. But Dr Akhtar simply pressed herself back in her seat. "We'll be entering the atmosphere soon. The pod is designed to withstand it."

"Eh?" said Mr Thark, but already they could hear it, the whining and whistling sound, and they could feel, too, the buffets and jolts that hit them. All at once it was around them and in them. The sounds increased, not only the sound of the air, but also the creaks and groans of the craft itself like an old ship straining in a storm and on the verge of ripping itself apart. Then Jenny noticed it was getting warmer.

It was her chair. It was the wall of the craft, from which she could now feel waves of heat radiating. It was the air itself. At first it was just a pleasant glow, but she could feel the temperature rising almost between breaths, and without warning the thought came to her: "Are we going to bake alive?" She heard a voice cry out, "Oh my God!" and she wondered if it was hers.

"It's just the atmosphere!" Dr Akhtar's voice said, loud and not quite calm. "Friction causes heat! It's all according to plan!"

What followed was a scene of hell, of heat and grinding judders and the high wailing of the air and the groaning of the straining structure in which they sat passive and helpless and Mr Thark's voice toneless and seemingly involuntary which repeated without end: "God in heaven God in heaven God in heaven God in heaven God in heaven God in heaven God in heaven God in heaven God in heaven..."

The little pod called Joyride screamed across the skies and came, quite according to plan, down to earth.

CHAPTER FIFTEEN: Journey's End

Afterwards, her memory of what had happened was fragmentary. She could see moments, vivid to the point of fever, but without any feeling of how they were linked. She could only guess at some sort of order.

The pod was cool again. They were rocking and bobbing inside the tiny space, too stupefied to consider any course of action. She could hear a sound like water lapping against the hull. In recollection, she supposed that Dr Akhtar must have had the presence of mind to activate the parachutes for the final drop, but she had no memory of that at all.

There was an argument as to whether they should open the portal. She did not know how that episode ended.

There was silence and sickness and groaning.

She felt as if there were something invisible but incredibly heavy pressing down upon her.

She did not remember the pain, but she did remember thinking: this is agony.

She also remembered another thought: if I die soon, at least this will be over.

And then, there was the memory of the portal opening and the air coming in and the momentary blocking of the light as Miss Jones climbed out.

She was lying on a broad expanse, pebbles under her, staring straight up at something which puzzled her very much. The thought came to her: is that what they mean by a cloud?

After this, the memories started to join up.

They were stumbling up the bank of smooth pebbles.

"Is this a beach?" she was asking.

"Yes," said Miss Jones.

"I thought they were made of sand."

"Not all of them."

Then there was a street. It was quite deserted except for the three of them, walking down the middle line and cautiously looking all around into the dark squares of the doors and windows and down every side street. The strand of the beach, and then the sea, were to their right, beyond a rail. Bushes sprouted out of the kerbs and through the cracks in the paving stones. Every so often they saw a car or a van standing by the side of the road, its windows smashed, its tyres down, its paintwork flaked and faded. There were signs, written in English, offering such tempting delights as Tea, Coffee, Buns, Ice Cream, Rock, Fudge, and Amusements (whatever they might be).

The sounds were of their feet, and of the harsh cries of the gulls, and the eternal, rhythmic and somehow soothing growl of the sea.

What there was not, anywhere, was any indication of existing human life. The shops and houses were long deserted. The cars and vans had been abandoned for uncounted years. The streets were silent and still and empty.

What Jenny remembered next was a procession of images: street upon street of emptiness, in monotonous, endless, awful succession; along with the feeling of weariness from her feet upwards which was slowly bringing her closer and closer to tears.

"Where are we going?" she asked. "Can't we stop?"

"We need water," Dr Akhtar said.

Jenny realised her lips were parched and that the ache in her body was, above all, a cry of thirst. She nodded hopelessly.

"But where are we going?"

The street was wider now, and the buildings did not loom over them so much. They passed over a great junction which was a roundabout. Each of the roads leading to it was divided into lanes to regulate the great traffic for which it was built. The central island had grown into a small forest. The pavements too were overgrown, and the rustle in the grass held a promise of rats. They stayed, therefore, in the road itself, and on the far side of the junction trudged up the fast lane at a steady two and a half miles an hour. It stretched away from them in a straight line to the horizon.

"Over the brow of the hill. That's where we're going."

Next there was a path stretching away from the wide road, cut through a wood. This path, too, was overgrown, but it was passable. They started down it, moving from bright daylight into a bosky darkness, a thick canopy of branches arching over them. There were dry stone walls on either side of the path, slightly too high for comfort. They walked in a line. Each held the shoulder of the one in front. The path was rough, and it was easy to stumble, but they came to no great harm.

They walked out the other side into the sudden sunlight, and they saw before them, at the top of that ridge, the great expanse of a vale, curved and green and luscious.

The sight smote Jenny and she could not move. She had never seen so far, never seen so much in one glance, never seen anything so beautiful. And it was then that she could take no more, and she sat in the mud of the path and cried. It was only later that she learned that the others had also sat, also cried. This was, to all of them, the moment they knew they had come home.

When she felt better, she looked around, and she saw that Miss Jones was standing again, and staring down into the valley.

"There's a river," she said.

They had to tread a path down the hill through the grass, which at times came up to their chests. Mr Thark and Miss Jones went first, as they were the ones who had memories of Earth, and who knew the perils and pitfalls of long grass. To Jenny, it all felt like a vivid dream, with a dream's combination of detachment and foreboding.

Now they were on the shore of a river, which ran shallow and sparkling over rocks and between heavy banks of trees. Miss Jones was first to scoop the water in her hands and to throw it into her mouth and over her face. The others followed. Jenny was shocked awake by the water's cold and outrageous impact. She paused, then scooped more into her mouth, greedily like a child.

She was sitting on the river's green verge, her head and upper body drenched in water. They felt revived, and they talked with the brittle energy of people who, using their last reserves, will very shortly find they have nothing at all left.

"Have you noticed something?" Mr Thark was saying to her. He was seated next to her in an awkward half-crossed-leg position which he would surely regret.

"What?" said Jenny.

"Look," he said. He pointed back at the field behind them. She looked.

"What?" she said.

"Which way did we come down?"

"That way, of course," she said, pointing at the path they had trodden through the grass, a dark line down the hillside.

"So what's that, then?" he said. It took Jenny a moment to see it, further down the field. It was another dark line in the grass.

"Animals?" Jenny suggested.

"Maybe," said Mr Thark.

Later, the realisation came to them that they needed food. They also realised that they had no idea how to get it.

"The grass," said Miss Jones. "That's edible."

"But not what you would call *tangy*," Mr Thark said.

"You have a better idea?" said Miss Jones.

"What about these?" Mr Thark said, walking up to a bush bearing bright red berries. He stretched out a hand to pick them, when a strange voice behind them called out:

"I wouldn't if I were you."

They turned, startled, and a tall, lean man stepped out of the woods.

CHAPTER SIXTEEN: The Village at the End of the World

THE MAN, WHOSE NAME WAS Ian, accompanied them to the village. He set out in considerable physiological detail exactly why it was a bad idea to eat the berries, and suggested they might prefer to join him for dinner back home.

His face was dark and lined, and his hair was a rough shock of greying locks. He said he was in his thirties, but he looked much older. He wore layers of old clothes, roughly stitched and darned where they had torn too badly. His feet were swathed in rags.

"Yes, I thought I saw something in the sky a couple of nights ago," he said, once they had explained their presence. "What's it like on the Moon these days?"

The village was a small settlement of eighteenth and nineteenth century cottages clustered round a small and undistinguished church. People had lived on that site since the thirteenth century. There were more recent additions to the dwellings too: half-wrecked caravans, tents, even sheets of corrugated iron propped on piles of bricks.

The street was quiet, but Jenny did see a pale face look out at them from one of the caravans. They were led, still dazed and weak from their journey, to a large building. As they passed the gate Jenny saw that it was called the Hall.

The man called Ian pushed the door open and called out. Next, there were kind faces, and they were led to a room where mysteriously and seemingly without transition they were given beds and food and hot drinks. It was a sudden time of rest and ease, and the next thing was falling backwards into sleep without dream or disturbance.

Over the next two days, they slowly recovered in the Hall, which, as it turned out, was a kind of makeshift hospital used mainly for the assistance of new arrivals. Jenny, Miss Jones and Dr Akhtar were in one room and Mr Thark in another. The women were visited by people whom they came to recognise, who brought meals and talked with them and allowed them slowly to build up an idea of the world they had fallen into.

The village was a ragbag community of those who had survived. One of the nurses, Susan, told them something of what had happened on Earth after the ships had left for High Hants. She spoke briefly of scorching summers, of droughts and floods, toxic fogs, ruined harvests, of breakdowns in the supply chain, of famine and riots, and of death, much death. What they went through had aged them, and made them tough.

"You soon learn," she said, "what you will do to stay alive."

The tale was soon told. Susan visibly avoided giving details. After a time, once death had ravaged everywhere she knew, the very worst, it seemed, was over. The fogs faded. Those who remained banded together. They pooled what little knowledge they had of the cultivation of crops and livestock. The village formed. The summers still burned, and there were still times of thirst. But ways could be found of surviving even these.

Life in the village was hard. Jenny realised that she would be expected to work, in the fields or the farmhouse or the yard. The Jenny she knew, who had been brought up on the Moon to be sweet and loving and essentially soft, recoiled from the thought. But she also knew, now, that there was more than one Jenny inside her. Jenny was harder than she thought, and wilder too. Yes, she would be fine, in the end, perhaps.

One day, they rose and dressed, and they ventured out into the village. It was a bright and warm morning, and the faces that turned to them curiously were many. These faces were of all colours too, to the confusion of Jenny who had lived so long among those that were exclusively white and pink.

"Oh, brave new world, that has such people in it," Mr Thark murmured. Miss Jones looked at him doubtfully.

A little man, round and ruddy-complexioned, was walking the other way down the street, a fishing rod over his shoulder. He stopped, seeing the group of strangers, and stared.

"Thark?" he said, astonished. "You here?"

Mr Thark stopped in his tracks. "Good God!" he cried. "Is it you?"

They approached each other with caution, and with a sudden glad cry came together and shook hands delightedly. "Bernie Barker! What the devil are you doing here? Jenny, this is Bernie Barker, you remember Bernie Barker, I told you about him. The police took him away for the sake of his Jerome K. Jeromes and his Miles Kingtons, and how he comes to be here is more than I can... Oh," he said, suddenly seeing it all. "Dr Popkiss chose you to come down, just as she chose us."

"I know," said Bernie Barker happily. "Isn't it a riot?"

The two were instantly off on a journey of reminiscence.

Later, the visitors were shown the fields, where horses pulled heavy ploughs across the dry soil and sowers broadcast their seed, and they knew this would be their own task soon.

The days passed. They learned their new place in the village. They became part of its rhythms and duties. Dr Akhtar guided a plough, Jenny kneaded bread, Mr Thark and Miss Jones sowed seed.

In spite of the welcoming arms they had found, and in spite of all the village's assistance, Jenny might not have coped if Dr Akhtar had not been there alongside her, the only other soul to whom the planet was quite new. At the end of each day they would retire to a quiet corner, Jenny and Parveen, talking together of the crazy world they had fallen into with its winds and weathers and its infinite skies, reassuring each other, helping each other through another turn of the Earth.

A couple of times a week, the four of them visited the inn, which was called the Inn, to sample its rough, refreshing beer or its sharp apple juice, and to draw breath in an atmosphere of nonsense and irresponsible gossip.

One night at the Inn, Mr Thark was in his element as usual, holding forth to the group. There was a sudden lull in the hubbub, and a vicious little phrase rang out from Mr Thark's lips loud and clear. He fell silent, but too late.

The landlord, a large black man called Joe Clayton, wandered out from behind the counter, without hurry or drama. The locals were already talking again in low tones, pretending with all their might to have noticed nothing. Joe approached their table, an easy smile on his face, and casually crouched by Mr Thark's chair.

Jenny, who was sitting next to Mr Thark, looked at the landlord's face and was startled to see in his eyes a look of pure hatred. In a moment it was gone and once more there was only the smile.

"Now, sir," he said quietly, but not too quietly for the others to hear, "you're an old man, and you're just back from the Moon, aren't you?"

Mr Thark nodded.

"And I hear they do things differently there. So I'm just going to tell you something nice and quiet and easy, and once. Don't let me hear you saying anything like that ever again. You hear me? Because if I do, I will smash your face in and send you right back to the infirmary, and don't you go thinking I am joking, because I'm not. Okay?"

Mr Thark nodded again.

"Good. Now what can I get you?"

And the hubbub slowly returned and the incident, it seemed, was over.

Later, Jenny left early, as she usually did, and as she went outside she saw, standing in the courtyard and staring into the night, Joe's daughter Helen.

Jenny stood alongside her. "Even the darkness in this place is beautiful," she said.

"Yes."

Jenny glanced at her impassive face and thought she saw in it something of what the other was thinking. "Mr Thark," she ventured, "he says these things, but he doesn't mean them."

Helen turned at that. "Yeah? Well, he won't mind not saying them then, will he?"

There was an awkward silence. At last, Jenny said, "I'm sorry."

"Sure," said Helen in a kinder tone.

They looked into the blue night for a while. Helen went on:

"It's just that Dad remembers it happening. I mean, what, all those years ago, when they, these rich white guys, just fucked off to the moon, sorry, in their big shiny spaceships. Just leaving us here to fucking die, sorry again, you know?"

"I'm sorry," said Jenny again.

"Dad's a good man," said Helen. "Forgiving. But he hasn't forgotten."

Jenny said, "I was only two."

"Yeah," said Helen. "That's right."

Jenny went back to the Hall and slept soundly. It was only on the following morning, when, passing Mr Thark's door, she saw his face, that she realised the night's events had not ended when she left the Inn.

His right cheek was livid and swollen, blooming in purple and black, and his lip had split open with a grim red slash. The nurse Susan was applying a small fabric plaster to the lip.

"What happened?" Jenny exclaimed, staring at him from the door.

Susan looked up. "Didn't you hear? I thought the racket must have woken up the whole village. He's been..."

"A naughty boy?" Mr Thark suggested with a conscious twinkle.

"An idiot," Susan corrected him coldly. "You should be ashamed of yourself."

She left a minute later, refusing to respond to his rueful smile.

"What happened?" Jenny repeated when she had gone.

"Well, you heard. I've been an idiot and I should be ashamed of myself. That seems a fair summary. Were you there when Joe had a word with me?"

"He was very reasonable, I thought, in the circumstances. Surely that was the end of it?"

"Oh, it was, for the moment. We had a few more jars after you went. I like his beer. It has a rough edge but a good heart. You know my lads, do you?"

"Your lads? Oh, you mean your new friends, Bob and Jim and, what are their names? I'm not keen on them, to be honest."

"They're not so bad really. They seem to have taken to me rather. What don't you like about them?"

"I think they're cruel."

"Come, that's harsh. Rough rustic humour, that's all. Also they laugh at my jokes. Well, it was throwing-out time and we were heading off, and Joe was just behind us making sure of it, when I happened to pass a comment, a mere nothing, about mine host's black looks, and...."

"Mr Thark!" Jenny exclaimed, shocked.

He shrugged. "It had to be said."

"No, no, it did not."

"Artistically, yes, it did, and, whatever else I am, I am an artist. It was the punchline, the necessary final tap. Don't you see I had no choice? Well, almost before the words were out of my mouth, I felt his hand on my shoulder and my body whirling round and blow after blow raining down on me, and I could hear a succession of shouts and inarticulate cries, and I honestly couldn't tell you if it was Joe or me that was uttering them. I don't think it lasted long, though heaven knows it was long enough. I found myself on the ground in what they call a world of hurts, and Joe hauled me up by the arm and held me up and brought me back to my room and threw me on the bed and left me, the swine. I could have died for all he cared."

Jenny shook her head. "I don't understand you at all. Sometimes you are so clever and full of understanding, but other times, like now, you just seem so... stupid. You're a disgrace. I'm sorry." And then, quite suddenly, she turned and left the room.

It was on the morning after that that Jenny, waking after her usual time, glanced over at Parveen's bed and saw her seated on its edge, intently looking down at a device which Jenny instantly saw was part of the equipment they had brought from High Hants.

"What is it?" Jenny asked, sitting up, though she knew the answer.

"I'm supposed to be reporting back," said Parveen. She toyed with the transmitter without switching it on.

"Are you going to?" Jenny asked.

"If I tell them how it is here," said Parveen, "if I tell them people are living and thriving, what will they do? Will they all come here? Isn't that what it's all about?"

"I don't know."

"It must be."

"Don't you want them coming?"

"No," said Parveen with sudden vehemence. "I do not."

"But are you going to disobey your orders?"

"I don't know."

Later, Parveen saw Mr Thark's friend Bernie Barker, sitting by the river, the line of his rod plunged in the water. She came over and joined him.

"What did you do?" she asked. "Did you ever report back?"

He glanced at her and an enigmatic expression crossed his face. "What do you think?"

She thought long and hard, staring into the ripples of the current.

"I think," she said slowly, "I think you took a big stone and smashed the transmitter over and over until there was nothing left."

"That's good thinking, that is," said Bernie Barker.

She stood up and, after some consideration, selected a stone from the river bank and hefted it in her hand. She nodded to herself and headed up towards the village. Bernie Barker smiled and turned his attention back to the line.

Soon after, the team that looked after the Hall let it be known that they considered the four newcomers were well enough to move out. They mentioned that a caravan was available in Magnus Field.

"Change and decay in all around I see," sighed Mr Thark, surveying the little room at the Hall that had been his home for almost two weeks.

They looked over the caravan, a rusty exhibit, its tyreless wheels wedged with bricks. "Cramped for four," said Mr Thark.

"Especially," said Miss Jones, "when one of them is a man."

A curtained corner for Mr Thark was suggested. "Hmm," he said. "Isn't there anywhere else I can go?"

After some inquiry, it was found that a family living nearby under a sheet of corrugated iron by the wall had a spare place, as their grandfather had died.

"It's not too bad," the son said. "You hardly get wet at all, even when it's pissing it down."

"Well," said Mr Thark. "Thank you. I'll think it over."

Later, when Jenny was passing his room, she saw him packing a rucksack. "You're taking up that offer?" she asked.

Mr Thark looked up. "Oh, so you're talking to me again?"

She smiled, a little tightly. "It seems silly not to, though I still think you're a disgrace."

"Thank you very much."

"Well, are you? Going to take up the offer?"

"No," he said. "I've decided to move on."

"I'm sorry?"

"I don't fit in here," he said, touching the still swollen side of his face, and went on lightly, "Can you see me as the ploughman homeward plodding my weary way? I'm a city boy."

"Are there cities any more?"

"That's something I need to find out. And besides..."

"Yes?"

"Well, I'll tell you. For twenty years there's been this canker inside of me, this regret that when I chose my books I chose the wrong ones. I always wanted my chance to go back and choose again. And now, you see, by some miracle I have that chance. I need to go and find the rest of my library."

"It'll be ransacked."

"Yes."

"You saw the town. Everything's smashed up."

"Yes."

"And that's just a little seaside town. What makes you think London will be any better?"

"I know, I know. Do you think I haven't thought all this? I just have to go, and that's all there is to it. After all," he added wryly, "it's not as if I'll be missed."

She wandered over to the window and looked unseeingly out at the overgrown churchyard opposite. "No," she said.

He asked, "What about you? Don't you want to find your mother?"

"No."

"Really? I thought..."

"Yes. So did I. But you see, I was at the Inn a couple of nights ago, and I got talking to, I think it was Janet. She's called Hodges, and she asked what my name was, and I told her. And she said, any relation to Martha Threadneedle? So I said, that's my mum. And she said to me... well, she said Martha Threadneedle had been part of the team, a sort of provisional government, who tried to hold things together when the crisis came. She's well spoken of apparently. But she didn't make it through. There was a virus. She died about fifteen years ago. So you see, there's no point looking for her. She's gone."

"I see."

Mr Thark completed his packing. He had acquired few spare clothes, and Jenny was at a loss to think what else could be in his pack, aside from his precious *Alice*; but she forbore to ask.

He stood up and hoisted the bag onto his back.

"Will you be all right here?" Mr Thark asked.

"Of course, why not?"

97

"Well. You were raised on the Moon. It's bound to be a shock, coming here."

"I'm getting used to the gravity. And at least we don't need to wear the boots down here."

"I don't mean that. I mean... you're coping with the people?"

"Why wouldn't I? I'm not such a sensitive plant as you think, Mr Thark."

"That's not what I meant."

"I know what you meant," said Jenny.

And there it was, back again, the unspoken thing, standing between them. She knew the kind of things he thought, because, heaven knows, he had never flinched from saying them. She watched his bruised face which he held aloft like a proud banner. He thrived, she knew, on outrage, on opposition. She could not understand this, the sheer stupidity of it. Why hate, why be hated, why wish those things on yourself? In the end, she and he were opposites. And yet he, himself, was not hateful, not really. It was an odd thing, and she sat in the room's one chair and tried to make sense of it.

"Isn't it strange," she said at last, "how we can understand things we've never seen? Yes, I grew up in High Hants where everyone was, well, white. And yes, I do feel awkward here sometimes, like a cat in a strange room. Where did that come from? I've never seen a cat. It must have been in a book. But that's just because I'm a bit foolish sometimes, and I can't help it. And the thing is, deep down in here" (she touched her head) "I know none of it makes a scrap of difference, where you came from, what colour you are, any of that. Maybe that's only book learning too, and sometimes I think it's not enough. It can only have come from books because God knows it didn't come from High Hants. Maybe every great writer has that little bit of knowledge in them, even when they fall short in what they write and for a moment the petty and mean side comes uppermost. And I think you have that knowledge too, though you try so hard to betray it. Well, I don't know. I'm young and I don't know anything. But then again, maybe everyone's the same in that too, just a child pretending to know things. I think... why am I preaching to you, of all people? How silly... I think all we can do is go through life as well as we can, tripping over ourselves and making ourselves look stupid, and maybe sometimes hurting people on the way without meaning to, but all the same *trying*. Don't you think?"

Mr Thark was leaning against the wall, his eyes closed, listening.

"Well," he said, "it's a point of view."

At last, he opened his eyes. "Come on, you can see me off."

It was late afternoon, fine and gorgeous, and the blue of the clear sky was deepening. "You should wait till tomorrow morning," said Jenny.

"No, I should go now," said Mr Thark. "It's time."

"What will you do tonight?"

He made an airy gesture. "Something will turn up."

"What makes you think that?"

"It always has." He considered for a moment. "It's odd. Perhaps you won't believe me, but I really am one of those who travel hopefully. And who would doubt the world's kindness on a day like this?" He grinned, and started to dance a foolish little caper in the road. "Will you walk a little faster," he half-sang in a peculiar voice, "said the whiting to the snail, There's a porpoise close behind us and he's treading on my tail. See how eagerly the lobsters and the turtles all advance, They are waiting on the shingle – will you come and join the dance?"

He stopped, and looked around to see if had been seen. The street was perfectly quiet. He shrugged, and hefted his bag.

"Forgive me," he said. "Call it something in the air. You see, I'm back on Earth, and at last I am free!"

They walked along the road for a minute.

"Won't you at least say goodbye to the others?" said Jenny.

"No. They don't care about me, and I certainly don't care about them. I don't make friends easily, you know."

"I know," she said, and felt a moment of strange sadness.

They were on the edge of the village. The buildings ended and the untrimmed hedgerows began. "This is where I leave you," he said. He held out his hand, and with a hesitation Jenny shook it. "Goodbye," she said. "Goodbye," he said, and turned and walked away.

She watched him depart with a jaunty step she had never seen in him before. She heard him softly singing as he strode into the distance. "Will you, won't you, will you, won't you, will you join the dance? Will you, won't you, will you, won't you, won't you join the dance?"

His figure disappeared round a bend in the lane.

Jenny turned back and was about to return to the village; but then she stopped on that spot and took in the things she saw. Really, this was a most beautiful place, after all. The dark old buildings and the waving green-clad branches were set against a blue sky like the blue of nothing but itself, and hanging there in that sea of nothingness above there was the creamy circle of the Moon, Jenny's old home, its face set in an expression of permanent surprise.

END

Other novels, novellas and short story collections available from Stairwell Books

The Iron Brooch	Yvonne Hendrie
Pandemonium of Parrots	Dawn Treacher
The Electric	Tim Murgatroyd
The Pirate Queen	Charlie Hill
Djoser and the Gods	Michael J. Lowis
The Tally Man	Rita Jerram
Needleham	Terry Simpson
The Keepers	Pauline Kirk
A Business of Ferrets	Alwyn Bathan
Shadow Cat Summer	Rebecca Smith
Shadows of Fathers	Simon Cullerton
Blackbird's Song	Katy Turton
Eboracvm the Fortess	Graham Clews
The Warder	Susie Williamson
The Great Billy Butlin Race	Robin Richards
Mistress	Lorraine White
Life Lessons by Libby	Libby and Laura Engel-Sahr
Waters of Time	Pauline Kirk
The Tao of Revolution	Chris Taylor
The Water Bailiff's Daughter	Yvonne Hendrie
O Man of Clay	Eliza Mood
Eboracvm: the Village	Graham Clews
Sammy Blue Eyes	Frank Beill
Margaret Clitherow	John and Wendy Rayne-Davis
Serpent Child	Pat Riley
Rocket Boy	John Wheatcroft
Virginia	Alan Smith
Looking for Githa	Patricia Riley
Poetic Justice	P J Quinn
Return of the Mantra	Susie Williamson
The Martyrdoms at Clifford's Tower 1190 and 1537	John Rayne-Davis
The Go-To Guy	Neal Hardin
Abernathy	Claire Patel-Campbell
Tyrants Rex	Clint Wastling
A Shadow in My Life	Rita Jerram
Rapeseed	Alwyn Marriage
Thinking of You Always	Lewis Hill
How to be a Man	Alan Smith

For further information please contact rose@stairwellbooks.com
www.stairwellbooks.co.uk
@stairwellbooks